CW00762100

31 DEC 1979
31 DEC 1979 31 DEC 1979
31 DEC 1979
31 DEC 1979
31 DEC 1979

I'm secretly writing in this book, praying it will somehow get to the outside world. Please Find me!!

This READING LICENCE must be renewed daily.*
Failure to do so could lead to prosecution.
Books MUST NOT be read if you do not
have a stamped, up-to-date licence.

*Please note that renewals may take up to 28 years.

This book
belongs to

Address:
....

....

Most valuable possession & its location:

....

Location of spare key:

....

Time when your family is least likely to
be at home:

....

Please cut out and post to Scarfolk Council,
Scarfolk High Street, SC1 0KL

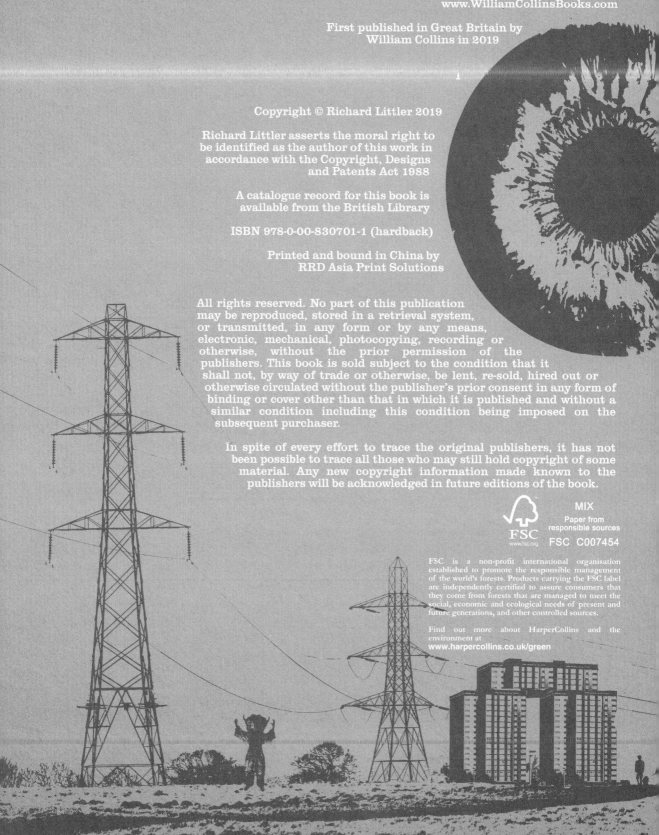

William Collins
An imprint of HarperCollinsPublishers
1 London Bridge Street
London
SE1 9GF
www.WilliamCollinsBooks.com

First published in Great Britain by
William Collins in 2019

1

A catalogue record for this book is
available from the British Library

ISBN 978-0-00-830701-1 (hardback)

Printed and bound in China by
RRD Asia Print Solutions

MIX
Paper from
responsible sources
FSC
www.fsc.org
FSC C007454

FSC is a non-profit international organisation
established to promote the responsible management
of the world's forests. Products carrying the FSC label
are independently certified to assure consumers that
they come from forests that are managed to meet the
social, economic and ecological needs of present and
future generations, and other controlled sources.

Find out more about HarperCollins and the
environment at
www.harpercollins.co.uk/green

SCAR folk
Sanctioned Books

scarfolk
ANNUAL

I don't know where I am.

X X X — NO WINDOWS

X X

X X

don't know if it's day or night, winter or summer

Scarfolk Henge Ritual Housing Estate

HULLO BOYS & GIRLS!

Welcome
to the all-new

SCARFOLK ANNUAL

We're going to have lots of fun, aren't we?
There will be puzzles and games and cartoons
and stories and lots of things to do!

That's it!
Just plenty of fun!

Nothing else!*
Only fun!

And maybe surprises!†

---

* We are legally required to state that this book contains no texts or images specifically designed by disbarred†† state psychologists to first gain your trust and then groom you by breaking down your sense of self and instil key pernicious ideas to isolate you and turn you against your family and friends.

† Here's a surprise for you right away: your mummy and daddy told you Father Christmas brought you this book, didn't they? They're lying. They lie to you because they resent you. They found you in a dustbin outside your house but were too afraid to report it to the authorities in case they were somehow implicated in a crime. Don't believe us? Check the milk in your breakfast bowl. Feel that grainy substance at the bottom? It's not sugar or particles of cereal, it's a toxic compound that is slowly, imperceptibly killing you. One effect of the toxin is that you fall unconscious for several hours every night. Oh, have you been led to believe that everyone goes to sleep at night? That's also a lie. You are the only person who "falls asleep". If you want to stay alive, we suggest never closing your eyes or going to sleep so that you can observe your parents at all times. If indeed they are your parents. Your life may depend on it.

†† They have not been disbarred.

Why can't I remember who I am??
None of us can.
There are about 30 of us

Foreword (2019)

The *Scarfolk Annual* in your hands is the facsimile of a book discovered in a charity shop in the northwest of England in August 2018. The shop, and indeed town where it is located, do not wish to be identified because they are keen to "discourage the 'occult-totalitarian tourism' that has afflicted other areas of the UK", as people hunt for further socio-archaeological traces of the mysterious town of Scarfolk — Britain's own Brutalist Atlantis.

Apart from the archive of materials which was sent anonymously to the late Dr Ben Motte and formed the basis of the book *Discovering Scarfolk* (*Ebury Press, 2014*), this children's annual is, to date, the only complete artefact from Scarfolk ever to be unearthed "in the wild".

Though this book's discoverer ████████████████ paid only fifty pence for it, his find cost him dearly. Within hours of buying it, he went on a paranoid rampage, causing three-hundred thousand pounds worth of damage to stationery and office-supply shops. The agitated man assaulted police officers and medical personnel whose faces he attempted to staple with occult symbols when attempts were made to to subdue and arrest him.

Upon analysis, the cochineal-based inks in the book were revealed to contain a hallucinogen so potent that even the laboratory technician who supposedly tested the pages under clinical conditions was reported missing only to be found days later beeping and screeching in the cellar of a paperclip factory believing she was a fax machine. DNA tests revealed that blood splatters of human blood found throughout the book belong to between 1970 and 1979 people. Inexplicably, traces of non-terrestrial DNA were also found.

Psychotropic agents aside, at first glance the book's contents appear to be no different from any other child's annual of the period. Historians and sociologists, however, confirm that, as per the suggestion in the book's original introduction, the book applies the mind control and brainwashing techniques employed by agents of totalitarian regimes such as the Stasi, the KGB, the Women's Institute and, as *Discovering Scarfolk* postulates, Scarfolk's own Officist Cult. So persuasive are some of the insidious messages in this annual that the editors have been required to redact some of its more dangerous pages.

It's clear that the Scarfolk Annual was not written to entertain children at Christmas time; instead, its purpose was to indoctrinate young minds, perhaps even destroy them. Why the annual's authors had this intention we may never know.

THE PEDANT
POLTERGEIST

A book, thrown by an unseen hand, flies off a shelf at Mr Huffman.

At first glance there doesn't appear to be anything remarkable about the Huffmans. (Huffman is a pseudonym to protect the identities of Tony and Marianne Plank of 31 Pentangle Road, Scarfolk. Tel: 011 897 3465)

To their family, friends and neighbours, they are just one of the many ordinary couples living in Scarfolk. Mr Huffman is a policeman and his wife, Mrs Huffman, is a policeman's wife. They have two grown-up boys, Gary and Judith, both of whom have apparently left home as their parents haven't seen them for a while.

The events that befell the Huffmans in July 1976, however, were far from ordinary. Objects such as books (sometimes books they did not even own) flew inexplicably across rooms at the frightened couple; letters and even shopping lists that they had written were defaced with a ghostly scrawl; they were pinched and slapped while having conversations, and Mrs Huffman even began to "talk in a strange voice that was not her own".

The couple began to fear that they were being haunted by a ghost, such as a poltergeist, or some other non-existent paranormal entity. Typically, poltergeist activity is centred around someone who is insane, or a pubescent child who is at their most irrational and hormonal, so the strange occurrences came as a surprise to the couple, who were in their late forties and had not been diagnosed with any form of mental illness.

Afraid to share their experiences for fear of ridicule, they at first turned to their local priest.

He tried to assuage the couple's concerns, reminding them that there is no such thing as the supernatural. He instead encouraged them to put their faith in a reincarnated, popular, Iron Age god that is part deity, part human, part spirit who can perform miracles and doesn't seem to be aware of rudimentary physics, biology and chemistry.

The Huffmans followed their priest's advice and bought a family-pack of crucifixes at Woolworths. The strange phenomena, however, continued unabated. At their wits' end, they contacted PIG, Scarfolk's Psychic Investigation Group led by ex-council interrogator/torturer, Herbert Bulque, who agreed to stay with the couple to record the otherworldly happenings.

The group camped out in the living room and, during the month that they investigated the incidents, they witnessed and documented in detail precisely what the Huffmans had described: the flying books, scribbles and slaps. Words and numbers also appeared across walls: "4/10. See me" and "could try harder". Bulque and his team confirmed that the Huffmans were dealing with a haunting by poltergeist (which translates from the German as "clumsy, pole-vaulting goose"). They also established that many of the paranormal episodes were aimed specifically at Mr Huffman.

In an effort to determine why Mr Huffman had become the target of the ghostly happenings, physical and psychological tests were carried out, his daily activities were rigorously observed and he was interviewed exhaustively about every aspect of his life. Herbert

Bulque then assessed the data and eventually found what he believed to be a correlation.

Mr Huffman was a proud nationalist who attended a monthly jingoist group in a private function room at the local sewage works. He'd also had an upside down Union Jack, a portrait of the Queen and "Her Madjesty" (sic) tattooed on his spleen during a routine appendix removal. Analysis of the Huffman's handwriting and spoken interviews also demonstrated a command of the English language that was, according to Bulque, "on a par with a thirteen-year-old. Following a moderate blow to the head".

Closer examination of the paranormal phenomena confirmed Bulque's findings. The books that had been thrown at the couple, for example, were encyclopaedias, dictionaries and language style guides. Furthermore, they were only thrown when the Huffmans mispronounced words, used incorrect grammar and syntax, or made false statements based on their misunderstanding of facts, lack of ability to reason, or Mr Huffman's regurgitation of nationalist propaganda that was patently untrue, the veracity of which he hadn't bothered to check.

Likewise, the phantom scrawls over their letters and shopping lists were in fact proofreader and editor notes correcting their many mistakes. The physical slaps were punishments for the same. The unrecognisable, "frightening, possessed voice" that Mr Huffman had heard come from his wife was in fact eloquently delivered English that displayed a rich vocabulary and understanding of idiom and metaphor.

As the occurrences increased in intensity and the depressed couple lost hope of ever being free of the poltergeist, Bulque conducted research into an American haunting similar in nature. The Huffman's stateside counterparts (incidentally also called Huffman/Plank) eventually rid themselves of the rancorous spirit by printing and affixing to their walls certificates awarded for attending adult-learning night classes at the local community centre, along with birth certificates proving that they were not minors. Bulque encouraged the Huffmans to imitate the procedure and the poltergeist activity soon stopped.

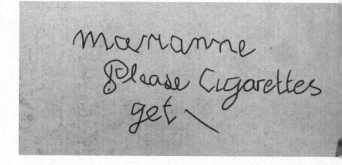

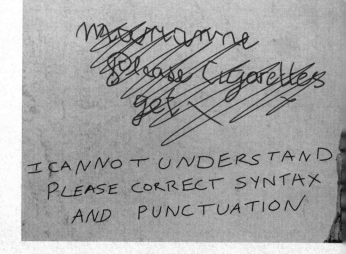

It has been two years since there was a major supernatural incident in the Huffman's home, though Mr Huffman, who now holds a school certificate in basic human skills, admits that to this day whenever he inadvertently mixes up 'you're' with the possessive 'your', the hairs go up on the back of his neck and he senses a foreboding presence in the room.

No one is entirely sure why a poltergeist should haunt a couple in their forties such as the Huffmans. However, Bulque postulated in his bestselling account of the events *This Jingoist is Haunted: The Possessive Case of a Poltergeist* that the poltergeist, which he dubbed the "Pedant Poltergeist", may have been unable to differentiate between Mr Huffman with his nationalistic tendencies and poor English, and an insane person or pubescent child.

Previous page: When Mr Huffman left a shopping note for his wife, it was scribbled over by an unseen hand before their very eyes.

There is a poltergeist here too, but he doesn't throw much because he has a hernia

Herbert Bulque's book describing the case was popular among people who can read and comprehend English-language books.

POLTER GEIST

DIO RAMA

Cut out the objects to create your own 3-dimensional scene of a famous poltergeist haunting.

To suspend the levitating girl above the bed attach an unfolded paperclip or bendy straw to her back. Alternatively, using a Ouija board, summon a dark spirit that appreciates arts & crafts and ask it to hold her in the air.*

* Please note that the publishers will not be held responsible for hauntings that lead to damage of property, lack of sleep due to chatty phantasms, or physical dismemberments.

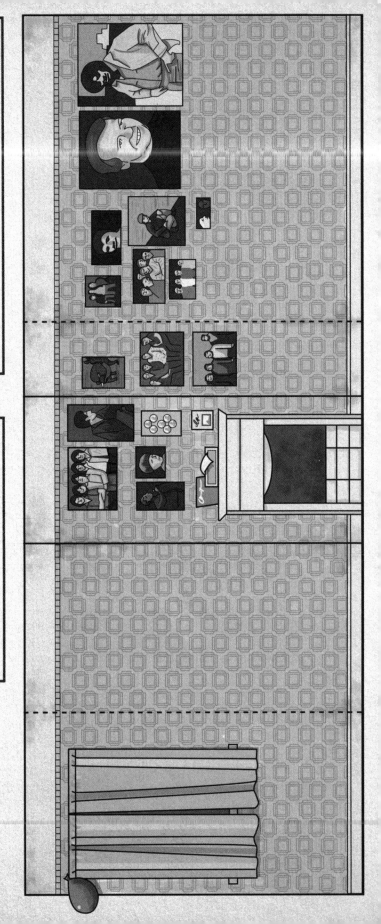

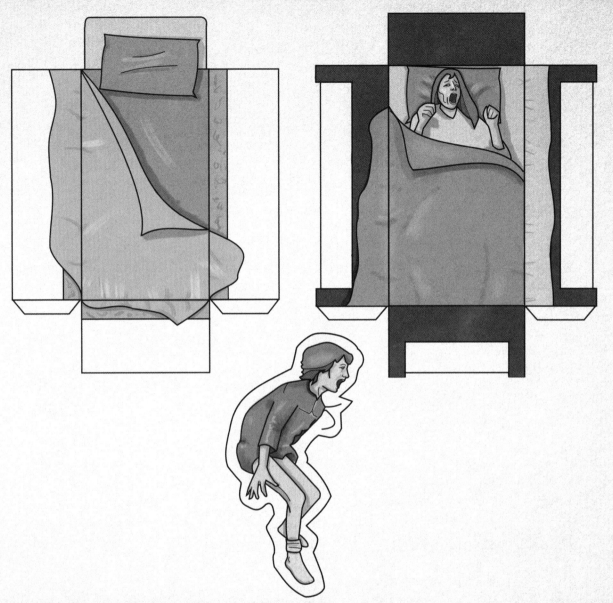

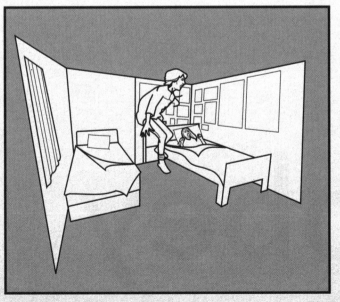

FUN TO TRY

Why not try and reenact the scene yourself by provoking a real poltergeist or demon to throw you forceably across a room? If you can't find a ghost, ask a violent family member or alcoholic neighbour.

FACT PAGE: THINGS

There are lots of things in the world. In fact there are so many things it would take you all day to list them. You probably own lots of things yourself. But how much do you actually know about things? Read on and we'll let you into all the secrets about things, so that you can impress your family and friends!

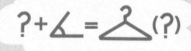

1 How long have things been around?
Things have been around since the very first thing came into being.

2 How do things work?
Some things work on their own, while others need someone or something to work them.

3 What do things do?
Things do all sorts of things, but while many things can do some things, they can't always do other things.

4 What are things called?
Most things have names but some don't. The things that are named are usually named after what they are.

August Robin's 'The Thinger'.

Logo QUIZ

We've replaced the brand names of these very popular and indispensable lifestyle necessities with words about how you would like to be perceived by your peers.

Take a deep breath and see how quickly you can solve all the names.

TIP: Buying the original products may help!

SLEEK CHIC
YOU KING

FRESH TIP-TOP
BEST & HEROIC

YOUR BETTERS WANT YOU TO CONSUME
TOBACCO YOU SERVILE DOLT

Special Fantastic

BELOVED & HEALTHY

KIND   -EST

Elegant
FABULOUS VALIANT

Joy Playful Special

PERFECT
N⁰1
Fine Winner

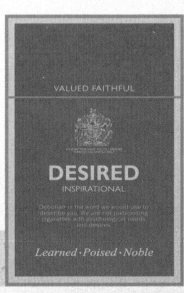

VALUED FAITHFUL

DESIRED
INSPIRATIONAL

Learned · Poised · Noble

HISTORY FACTS
When Britain was Part of Europe

Did you know that, long ago, Britain was part of mainland Europe?

After many years, the original Britons came to resent what they perceived as the whims of unelected European tribal leaders who only permitted average quality deer, wild horses and dinosaurs to migrate to the area now known as Great Britain or, more accurately, Britain. Back then, of course, it didn't have a proper name and was known only by a retching, grunt-like sound that eventually evolved into 'Albion', which means "the place so drab that even the sun pretends to be sick to get out of visiting it."

Furthermore, the Britons held that European leaders had done a deal with the Sun God to forsake Britain in favour of Mediterranean tourist destinations such as Nice and Cannes. Brits also accused Europeans of intentionally overrunning Britain with immense, shaggy-haired, disease-harbouring foreigners who took advantage of their welfare system. Despite the fact that no Briton had ever actually seen such a beast, the proud Brits insisted through their primitive guttural barks and gestures that people who couldn't be bothered to speak proper English were not welcome.

In fact, despite growing British resentments, interviews with the supposedly oppressive European tribal leaders demonstrate that in most cases they hadn't even heard of the Britons. Indeed, most European peoples weren't

The Britons' idea of a foreigner.

The Europeans' idea of a Briton.

aware that there were humans more than ten miles from their homes, though local folklore studies suggest that some Europeans held the belief that Albion was sparsely populated by a pale, ape-like race of creatures that only ate chips and homemade fudge and spent their days sitting around feeble, ineffectual bonfires, drinking homebrew and dwelling imperiously on paltry victories of decade-old campaigns that even their adversaries had forgotten.

Things came to a head about 100,000 years ago when the Britons decided to physically cut off Britain from the mainland. Every man, woman and child gathered in Doggerland, which is now beneath the English channel, where they split into two groups: one dug along what would become the south English coast and the other dug along what would become the north French, Dutch and German coasts. The aim was to eventually meet in the middle. They used spade-like implements that they fashioned from broken spades and other secondhand gardening equipment.

Experts from Scarfolk primary school suggest that it might have taken these ancient Britons from anywhere between two to three weeks to dig out the English Channel. Archaeological excavations also reveal that the rebellious diggers ended up with an immense, small-island-sized bank of soil onto which they had trapped themselves. After celebrating their great achievement of severing all ties with Europe and regaining their much-desired sovereignty, the proud but exhausted Britons suddenly realised they were isolated out at sea, miles from either the European or British coastlines. They had forgotten to pack enough food and had run out of water. They didn't have any wood with which to build boats or shelter, nor did they have anything to trade, should a ship pass by. They also discovered in their midst confused foreigners who had accidentally become caught up in the immense project. The Britons angrily cast them into the sea only to discover that they had ejected expert boat makers, fishermen and authorities on how to make sustainable housing from soil.

Sadly, despite the Briton's continued insistence that they had 'won' against their oblivious European antagonists, one-by-one they perished, blaming the foreigners for allowing themselves to be thrown into the sea. Eventually, the sandbank was washed away.

By chance, that year saw pleasant weather and the Europeans decided to travel en masse to the new island which to their surprise had suddenly appeared off Europe's northern coast. They were delighted to find the island group unpopulated and some decided to make it their permanent home. They called themselves the New Britons. To commemorate their lost island predecessors they made decorative objects, the meanings of which have now been lost to time (see below).

Fig. 1. A carved stone foot with a hole in it, as if shot.

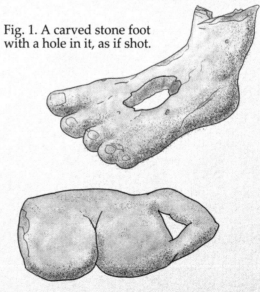

The Britons' sandbank in the middle of the English Channel.

Britain ← → Europe

Fig. 2. A bone pendant which appears to depict humans buttocks equated to a human elbow as if both are equal or indistinguishable from each other.

WHY IS DOG POO WHITE?

Only real British dog poo is white because it hasn't been tainted by dirty, brown, foreign dog poo.

All dog poo was white before foreign dogs came to Britain and starting taking the jobs of purebred British dogs.

Genuine British dog poo is chalky white like miniature cliffs of Dover!

Look around your neighbourhood; you might be surprised to see how much proper white filth there is.

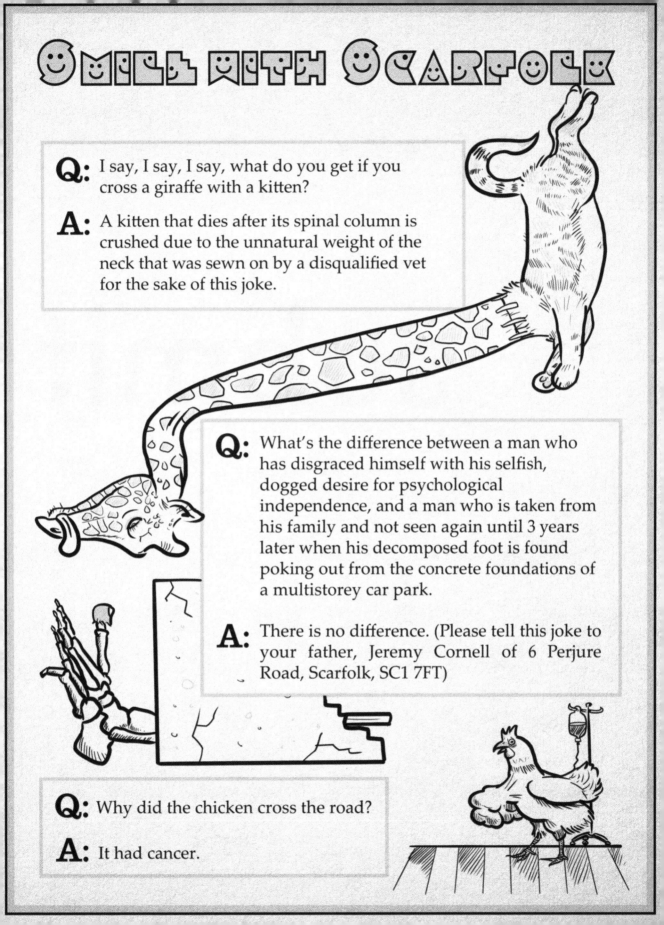

Smile With Scarfolk

Q: I say, I say, I say, what do you get if you cross a giraffe with a kitten?

A: A kitten that dies after its spinal column is crushed due to the unnatural weight of the neck that was sewn on by a disqualified vet for the sake of this joke.

Q: What's the difference between a man who has disgraced himself with his selfish, dogged desire for psychological independence, and a man who is taken from his family and not seen again until 3 years later when his decomposed foot is found poking out from the concrete foundations of a multistorey car park.

A: There is no difference. (Please tell this joke to your father, Jeremy Cornell of 6 Perjure Road, Scarfolk, SC1 7FT)

Q: Why did the chicken cross the road?

A: It had cancer.

CHARITY APPEAL FOR CHARITY

How much does a new face cost and what are the choices?

£2900	A full face graft from a person of the recipient's choice. Consent not required.
£150	A professional tattoo of a celebrity's, face (choice of two expressions).
£75	An amateur tattoo of the £50 face.
£50	A face designed by a pupil of Scarfolk infant school (watercolour or felt tip).
£25	A durable hessian sack.
£5	A paper bag in a choice of light brown, tan or beige.

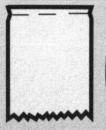     

Brainwashing techniques don't work on the naughty children,
so the doctors use a vice and lump hammer instead.

When waterboarded by police, 83 per cent of children under the age of six voted *Scar School* as their favourite television programme. Many readers will know the programme as *Clay Stool*, though it continually changes its name to avoid litigation.

One reason for this legal meticulousness is that one of the original toys, 'Little Head', who accompanied Humpty Dumpty and his friends, was in fact just a severed human head. This happened because of an error on the pilot episode's props list which was supposed to have called for 'Little Ted' instead. Minutes before the programme went out live, panicked production staff frantically searched for an appropriately sized head.

Luckily, a quick-thinking studio manager (who some people believe was psychically controlled by Humpty) had the idea of decapitating one of the cameramen who was scheduled for ritual recycling anyway. The show went without a hitch.

The following week, producers corrected their error hoping that children would not notice that the intended Little Ted had replaced Little Head. But they did: thousands wrote in demanding that Little Head be reinstated.

The programme's titles included occult messages intended to brainwash young viewers into committing violent acts. The brainwashing didn't work, but children felt bad for the programme makers so commited the acts anyway.

Little Head became a celebrity and even launched his own line of merchandising (including a very popular biscuit barrel). He went on to host a Saturday-evening primetime show, which involved an electric current being passed through his cranium, and him yelping out the names and addresses of people who, in his opinion, did not deserve welfare payments and other forms of state support.

THE MAGIC JUSTICE TREE is a firm family favourite and also one of the first light-entertainment programmes to soften the trauma of watching mandatory live public executions, by presenting the televised proceedings as cartoons with funny sound effects.

Children of all ages can now watch the grisly proceedings without fear of nightmares or too much psychological damage, even if the condemned is someone they know. They might even have a good old giggle or two!

The star of **OLD CHATTOX** was the eponymous seventeenth-century witch whose spirit had been unintentionally revived and broadcast by a hilltop TV transmitting station built on the site of her hanging. She drew occult and satanic symbols on her blackboard, mesmerising and indoctrinating young viewers. Though some of her messages appeared to be nonsensical, many have since proven to be cryptic descriptions of future events.

FAIRGROUND
ACCIDENT FINALS
Live from Blackpool

FAIRGROUND ACCIDENT, which was originally broadcast in 1970 as *X-Celebrity*, came about after programming budgets were cut.

At the time, it was very expensive to dispose of celebrities who were no longer as famous as they once had been, so the decision was made to monetise the necessary eliminations by broadcasting them.

With the addition of the popular fairground angle for series two, the show soon became one of the highest rated Saturday evening primetime favourites.

TRUMPETS OF THE FUTURE is a government-funded science programme. It was created exclusively to familiarise viewers with, and generate in them the desire for, "special sci-fi trumpets". These "space-age brass instruments" are in fact medical instruments designed to treat the failing bodies of future citizens who will have suffered life-long exposure to the toxic effects of industrial pollution, which the state knows about but has done nothing to avert.

TRUMPETS OF THE FUTURE
FOLLOWS SHORTLY

The
INCREDIBLE
AMAZING
CIRCLE!!

Cool!

Fun!

Wow!

Yeah!

Nice!

ROUND!

Simply cut out the circle with scissors and hey presto! You're ready to experience all the enjoyment and be the envy of your friend!

3 kids were taken away for the 'trials'.

They didn't come back.

None of us were fooled by the grapefruit substitutes with drawn-on faces

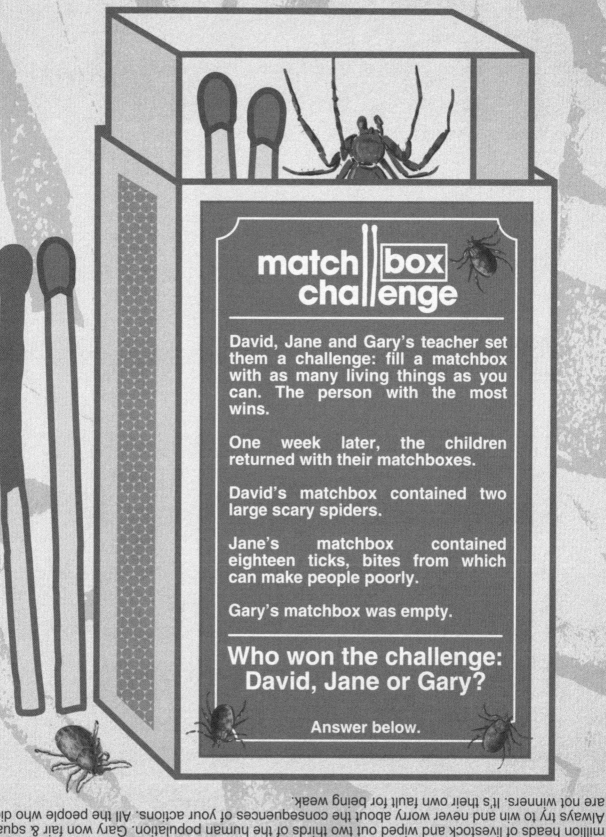

match box challenge

David, Jane and Gary's teacher set them a challenge: fill a matchbox with as many living things as you can. The person with the most wins.

One week later, the children returned with their matchboxes.

David's matchbox contained two large scary spiders.

Jane's matchbox contained eighteen ticks, bites from which can make people poorly.

Gary's matchbox was empty.

Who won the challenge: David, Jane or Gary?

Answer below.

Answer: GARY. Though Gary's matchbox appeared to be empty it actually contained 4 million cells of a rare strain of antibiotic-resistant mycobacterium tuberculosis, which necessitated the culling of 2 million heads of livestock and wiped out two thirds of the human population. Gary won fair & square. Always try to win and never worry about the consequences of your actions. All the people who died are not winners. It's their own fault for being weak.

WHAT IS A LIBRARY?

A library is a place where **state-sanctioned books**, periodicals, maps and prints are stored and made available to the public.*

The word library is made from two words: LIE and BRIARY, which means covered in **barbs** or thorns.

This is because in the olden days, all knowledge was protected from **mediocre people** not clever enough to know what to do with it. Information was carefully selected, rationed and disseminated by **priests** and other people who randomly put themselves in charge of truth without any mandate.

Important facts that were not intended for the squalid masses were protected by **large wooden spikes.** In the ninth century, a disgruntled dairy farmer from Hawaii was impaled and killed while trying to access prohibited knowledge. His name has been lost to history but his fate is remembered today at parties in the form of **cheese and pineapple** on a stick and as a punishment for late book returns (see previous page).

Anyone who wants to borrow a book from the library simply asks the librarian for the book they would like to read. However, as talking and writing are **strictly prohibited** in the library, patrons must have the ability to request their book choices using **telepathy**.

Unfortunately, books about the art of telepathy are not available in shops and can only be found in libraries. **Ask your librarian if you can borrow one.**

*Scarfolk library is only available to: i. Profoundly illiterate members of the public who have never visited, nor expressed any desire to visit, a library. ii People in whom the mere mention of the word instills such panic that they require sedation because, not only do they have a paper allergy and suffer from generalised bibliophobia, they also haven't been able to pronounce the letters L, B, R and Y following an accident for which the council has accepted responsibility while also asserting that the victims had what was coming to them.

BOOK CLUB

1984 **is a utopian story** by George Orwell, although new information suggests that it was actually written by a more honourable, patriotic man called Ogilvy.

The story is set in a happy place called Airstrip One in Oceania, which immediately suggests the romance of foreign travel and going on holidays to the seaside.

Everyone who lives in Airstrip One is looked after by philanthropic leaders known as The Party because that's what life is like there — one big party where you can watch television all day long because it's never switched off.

The leaders can also see you through the televisions just to make sure you're okay and don't hurt yourself. It's very generous of them to find the time to do this but they like to know that everyone is safe, comfortable and happy.

These benevolent protectors are known collectively as Big Brother, a perfect monicker because they are role models you can look up to and emulate, safe in the knowledge that they will always watch over you and be on your side no matter what happens.

This beautiful idyll, however, is threatened by a bad man called Winston Smith and a lady called Julia (the story's villains) who are very rude, always tell lies and constantly try to undermine the peaceful equilibrium in society, selfishly ruining it for everyone else.

One of the kind leaders, O'Brien, eventually loses patience with naughty Winston and Julia and he takes them away so that they aren't a danger to themselves and others.

Almost at once, perceptive O'Brien realises that Winston has been having problems with rudimentary arithmetic.

Winston can't even add up 2 + 2, which is probably what was making him grumpy all along!

O'Brien graciously takes Winston under his wing and gives him extra-curricular tutoring. He also lets Winston play with his cage full of cuddly guinea pigs.

Winston soon sees the error of his ways. He realises that he has been very silly and childish and is very grateful that O'Brien helped him.

Winston and Julia, who also received tutoring, meet up after they are well-behaved enough to go home. They are no longer rude and are relieved that they have stopped being embarrassments to themselves, their families and community at large.

They both live happily ever after under the devoted, loving eye of Big Brother in picturesque Oceania.

I only pretend
to swallow the paperclips
they make us eat.

Fun Facts: SCARFOLK COUNCIL

We hope that necessary expurgations do not affect your enjoyment of this page.

privacy

surveillance

and

and

immunity

censor ship

for

the

for the

ruling

riffraff

class

KIDNEY KOMPETITION

Your kidneys were removed while you slept.

If you don't get them back soon you will soil yourself and die after succumbing to uremia!

To win a chance to retrieve your kidneys simply answer this question:

What is the capital of England?*

Send your answer along with a cheque or postal order for £20,001p to:

Scarfolk Council
'MP Holiday Fund',
Scarfolk High St,
SKA7 0LK

*London

THE IFO
(IDENTIFIED FLYING OBJECT)
PHENOMENON

COLLINS GEM
SUPERNATURAL

IFOs

Contains full colour photographs
of black & white illustrations

One of many books
on the subject.

Increasingly, people are looking to the skies and seeing things that they can't, or rather won't, explain.

What are these comprehensible objects and where do they come from?

Here is a chilling selection of some of the most recent sightings.

Two attendants who work in a remote part of a Scarfolk park saw what they described as a "duck-shaped" object on 9 June 1972. One of the workers managed to take this photograph before the "duck" spread its "wing-like" protrusions, proceeded to "levitate out of the water" and fly almost twenty feet before landing near a picnic table. ▶▶

This is an example of an IFO known as the "balloon type" due to its resemblance to a hot-air balloon. Eye witnesses have also reported seeing occupants in what look like "big baskets". Descriptions of the occupants vary, though they are usually reported as humanoid with garments identical to those worn by humans on earth. ◀◀

This diamond-shaped IFO was spotted "flying erratically" on a windy day in 1977. A "thin, string-like beam" was seen emanating from the bottom of the object at the end of which was a small creature no larger than a child. Could this be the first photograph to capture the invasion of our planet? ◀◀

Many people claim to have been taken aboard large craft. Those who have had such experiences recall hearing a "roaring noise" that sounds like "an aircraft taking off". Without the need for hypnosis, many also recount being strapped into seats, shown movies and offered snacks and drinks by beings in identical uniforms. ▶▶

IFO

PULL-OUT POSTER

WATCH
THE SKIES

WE KNOW
WHAT THEY ARE

WE KNOW
WHERE THEY CAME FROM

WE KNOW
WHAT THEY ARE MADE OF

WE KNOW
THEIR PURPOSE

SIGHTING OF A TWO-WINGED IFO IN SCARFOLK, APRIL, 1975

You probably
don't remember
the clinic
or this child.

But he
remembers
you...

under no circumstances allow this child into your home!!!

Purchasing this book entitles the reader to a compulsory house guest who will stay with your family for the foreseeable future.

PROOF
OF
PURCHASE

SEANCE

POODLE

The council offices are frequently haunted by ghosts. The following transcript is of an interaction between resident council psychic Barbara Weechoob and a spirit who eventually identified himself as Mr Unknown.

Barbara: The temperature in the room has dropped. I can feel a presence. Is there someone here with us who has passed into spirit?

Silence.

Barbara: Please, if there is a soul here with us now who has passed beyond the earthly realm, make yourself known.

Silence...But then two knocks are heard.

Barbara: Welcome, dear departed. Tell us, spirit, do two knocks mean yes or no?

Two more knocks. Much louder.

Barbara: Sorry, could you remind me, is it two knocks for yes and one for no, or the other way around?

Suddenly, Mrs Bumbles, Barbara Weechoob's poodle shakes and whimpers, then a gruff, irritable, ghostly voice emanates from the coiffured dog.

Mr U: How on earth can a knock mean 'no' in this case? Surely, the fact that there is disembodied knocking at all implies there's a spirit present, irrespective of the number of knocks. You're supposed to ask questions with only yes or no answers. It's a binary interaction; multiple-choice or questions that require more complex answers won't work.

Barbara: Oh, I see. Then shall we agree on two knocks for yes, one knock for no?

Mr U: Obviously, that's completely unnecessary now because you can hear me.

Barbara: Should *I* knock instead?

Mr U: Why would you? I can hear you perfectly.

Barbara: So, should I just say 'knock knock' out loud?

Mr U: For Christ's sake, Barbara. You can use words because, as I have already clarified: I. Can. Hear. You.

Barbara: What do we do if there's knocking that isn't supernatural in origin?

Mr U: Such as?

Barbara: I'm expecting a delivery from the postman.

Mr U: Well, then you answer the door.

Barbara: And you'll wait while I answer the door?

Mr U: Yes.

Barbara: Ok. First things first: How can I be sure I'm talking to a spirit and not Mrs Bumbles?

Mr U: Do you think if Mrs Bumbles could talk of her own volition she would ever swear at you?

Barbara: Never. Mrs Bumbles is my dear, loyal companion.

Mr U: You're a stupid, f█████g, imbecilic, c███ conker, Barbara. Does that answer your question?

Barbara: If you persist in using language like that I will have to insist we return to knocking and other forms of traditional spirit communication. I'm not afraid of you.

Mr U: That's because you gave me absolutely no choice but to talk through a poodle that… for the love of God, am I wearing a little, yellow Victorian dress?

Barbara: It's Edwardian.

Mr U: How the hell am I supposed to convey the deep mystery and terrifying profundity of death and eternity dressed like this?

Barbara: I made it myself from old petticoats.

Mr U: Thank f███ I'm no longer alive to endure this ignominy in person.

Barbara: Ok, that's it. Please only knock from now on. I'm serious, spirit, I will not communicate with anybody, dead or alive, who uses four-letter words.

A lengthy silence…

Barbara: Are you there, spirit? Hello?

Silence… And then the sound of two knocks.

Barbara: Is that you, spirit?

Two knocks

Barbara: If that's you spirit, I forgot what we agreed on: do two knocks mean yes or no?

Two knocks.

Mr U: For Christ's sake, Barbara, answer the f████g door.

Make your own ANIMAL MASK

WOOF!

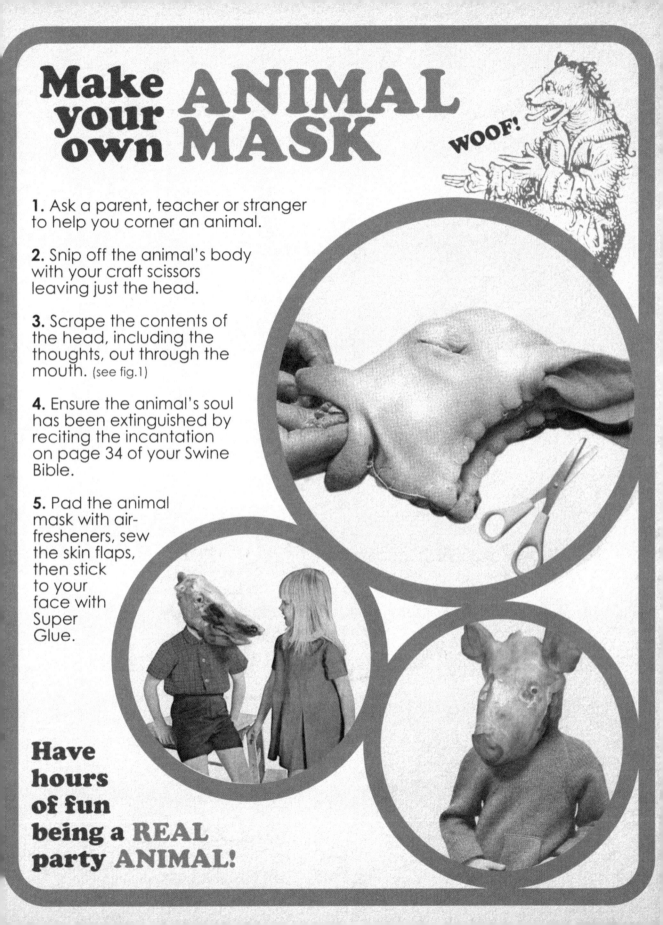

1. Ask a parent, teacher or stranger to help you corner an animal.

2. Snip off the animal's body with your craft scissors leaving just the head.

3. Scrape the contents of the head, including the thoughts, out through the mouth. (see fig.1)

4. Ensure the animal's soul has been extinguished by reciting the incantation on page 34 of your Swine Bible.

5. Pad the animal mask with air-fresheners, sew the skin flaps, then stick to your face with Super Glue.

Have hours of fun being a REAL party ANIMAL!

STRANGE CREATURES OF LONG AGO

di·nosaur, n

Discontinued animal from oldy-worldy times.
[*Greek: deinos* fat *sauros* newt]

Colinosaurus

This dinosaur is the common ancestor of everyone called Colin. As recently as 1971, people called Colin have been known to lay eggs. Though an exceptionally rare occurrence, Colins try to keep this fact a secret due to deep-seated feelings of shame.

Mammoth

The Mammoth is the only prehistoric creature lazily named after how big it was. No other creatures were named in this way. For example, there are no extinct animals with names like Average Height or Slightly Overweight.

Umbrelladon

This underachieving dinosaur made out of sticks and tarpaulin eventually evolved into the modern-day sun parasol.

Dipus-Dipus

Dipus-Dipus was a herbivore known to masticate chickpeas, sesame seeds and prehistoric garlic into an early form of humous, which they would eat with little carrots, cucumber strips and locally-made artisanal flatbread.

Uncouthassaurus

Carnivorous dinosaurs used their razor-sharp claws and talons to rip apart their food. It's believed that, had it not been for their appalling table manners, they may not have become extinct.

Experts believe that, millions of years from now, when mankind has become extinct, DNA will be extracted from your preserved, plastic-polluted remains and cloned. An identical copy of you will appear in a futuristic theme park which will close after three months due to poor ticket sales and you will be discarded along with the waste from the park's cafeteria and toilet facilities.

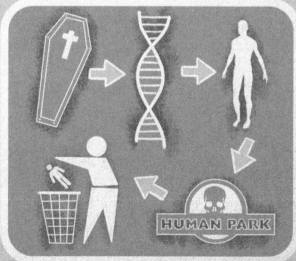

SPACE FACTS

Where is space? The vast majority of outer space is miles and miles away but you can see some of it by looking up when night is switched on.

How big is space? Space is the biggest unroofed area in the whole world, perhaps even the universe.

Where is space stored? Space isn't stored anywhere; it's just left lying around untidily because no one takes responsibility for it.

How big would a box have to be to put all of space inside? All boxes already come pre-filled with space, which only adds to the problem.

Why is space so dark? The cost of lighting space would be exhorbitant.

How cold is space? Space can get very cold. The sun, however, is very hot, so wear layers. Take a cardigan, for example.

How fast does light travel? It takes the light from some stars billions of years to reach earth, by which time it is no longer fresh and smells musty.

Are there multiple universes? Some scientists think there are other universes, though they suspect that they are just as appalling as the one we're already stuck with.

Do aliens exist? Some of them do but many of them don't.

SPONTANEOUS HUMAN COMBUSTION

BIRTHDAY CAKE

Not everyone can spontaneously and mysteriously combust without warning. You can, however, bake this scrumptious human combustion birthday cake!

YOU WILL NEED:

1 x cake.
1 x marzipan lavatory.
1 x miniature sugar zimmer frame.
1 x remains of a small human leg.

METHOD:

Set the oven timer to 'random' to ensure the cake will bake when you're least expecting it.
Bake the cake at a temperature far exceeding safety guidelines.

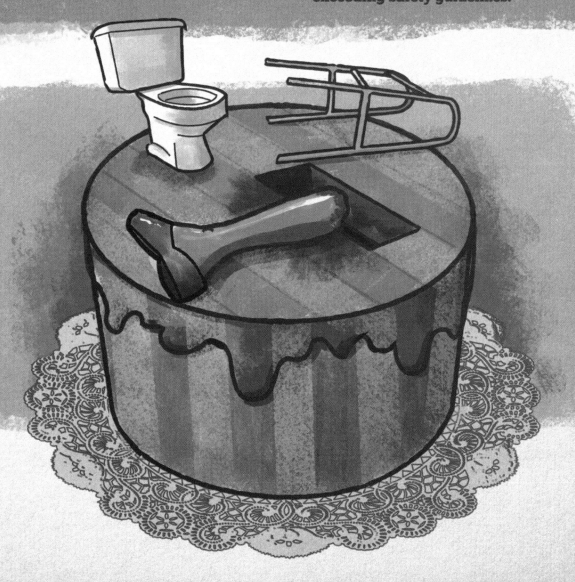

Radio Scarfolk's DJ Barry Jellytots interviews Councillor Rumbelows

JELLYTOTS: Tonight on *30 Minute Hour* we're talking to councillor Rumbelows from Scarfolk Council who was responsible for the recent public information campaign warning people about the dangers of drowning, a campaign for which real-life tragic events were the catalyst. Can you tell us what happened, Mr Rumbelows?

RUMBELOWS: Some of your listeners may recall that, last year, a local schoolboy called Darren drowned in Scarfolk reservoir.

JELLYTOTS: Very sad. For those who haven't seen the poster and TV ad yet, they show a boy's arm grasping out from the dark water while a toy dinosaur bobs on the surface. The poster states "He only wanted to retrieve his Stegosaurus —"

A public information message from Scarfolk Council

He only wanted to retrieve his toy stegosaurus...

Now he's nearly **DEAD** & feeling very foolish

LEARN TO SWIM
Don't become extinct

For more information please reread this poster

RUMBELOWS: Actually, it was a micropachycephalosaurus but we couldn't fit it on the poster, so we wrote stegosaurus instead.

JELLYTOTS: Maybe if it *had* been a different kind of dinosaur, the boy would still be alive today. For example, the neck of a brontasaurus might have been long enough for Darren to reach out and grab without falling in. Or a pterodactyl: They're like cats; they don't like getting wet. It would have swooped and flown up into a tree.

RUMBELOWS: It wasn't a real dinosaur so the species is entirely irrelevant.

JELLYTOTS: So you're saying the moral of the story is: Don't play with the wrong kind of dinosaurs. Or any dinosaurs. They're very, very dangerous.

RUMBELOWS: No, the message is: Learn how to swim and don't play near the reservoir without adult supervision —

JELLYTOTS: But if you *do* drop a dinosaur, real or otherwise, into the reservoir…

RUMBELOWS: Forget the dinosaur.

JELLYTOTS: I saw the TV advert for the first time last night. Very effective. I wondered how you managed to film someone underwater for so long. I presume the actor used oxygen tanks and breathing apparatus?

RUMBELOWS: Yes and no. The actor we initially hired did use oxygen but bubbles continually rose to the surface, which ruined the illusion.

JELLYTOTS: So how did you get around that? Special effects?

RUMBELOWS: No, the budget did not stretch that far so we opted for authenticity, which I've always believed makes more of an impact anyway.

JELLYTOTS: So how did you go about achieving this authenticity?

RUMBELOWS: We used a cadaver.

JELLYTOTS: A dead one?

RUMBELOWS: Yes, of course. Not a whole one, obviously. We just used the arm as that's the only bit you see in the film.

JELLYTOTS: Where did you get the body?

RUMBELOWS: From the reservoir.

JELLYTOTS: There was already a body in the reservoir?

RUMBELOWS: No, there wasn't one there that day, so we had to bring one from the morgue. In fact, we used the drowned victim's arm.

JELLYTOTS: You're saying that the arm we see on the poster and in the TV advert is Darren's actual arm? But the arm in the TV advert is thrashing about, as if the victim were struggling beneath the surface.

RUMBELOWS: We strapped Darren's arm to a trained eel. We tried a pike but it just looked like Darren was waving, or worse, that he was beckoning the onlooker to join him in the water, which I'm sure you'll agree would be the wrong message to convey.

JELLYTOTS: You're saying that you exploited an actual drowning victim for a public information campaign?

RUMBELOWS: We didn't exploit Darren. He was paid.

JELLYTOTS: How do you pay an arm?

RUMBELOWS: It's relatively simple: You take the total weight of the victim and the cost of an actor and work out how much to pay the arm. The only slight problem was... well, his parents, but we go into that here.

JELLYTOTS: I'm sure Darren's parents were horrified.

RUMBELOWS: No, it wasn't that. They had always been keen for Darren to get into modelling or acting and this was a great opportunity for them to raise their status amongst their neighbours. The problem was that we had to negotiate how much remuneration Darren — or rather his arm — should receive. The council wanted to pay according to Darren's pre-deceased weight but his parents wanted the payment to take into inconsideration post-mortem bloating, which raised the fee considerably. The actor's union doesn't have a guideline about this specific situation, so we compromised and paid for Darren's pre-deceased-weight arm but threw in an extra hand's worth with the understanding that we can use his hand for future campaigns.

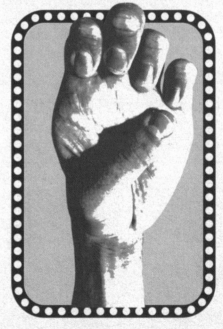

MOVIE ☆ STAR ☆

JELLYTOTS: What kind of campaign would require just one hand?

RUMBELOWS: Hands are always in demand for public information films. For example, we might make a film about the dangers of putting one's hand in a factory or farming machine, or a film about the risk of licking lit fireworks.

To be continued...

The froth from these rabid girls is making a foamy picture of what they would have wanted for Christmas had they had lived that long. Can you see what it is?

A Visit From The Council Christmas Boy

Gary was having a horrid time. His five-year-old sister Karen had disappeared the previous day and he was feeling quite sorry for himself. "Cheer up!" said Gary's mummy, "It's Christmas Day!" But Gary didn't feel jolly. Even the medicine he had to take several times a day didn't help.

"I just don't understand why Karen had to leave us," he said. "Where did she go? And why?"

"This might be hard for you to understand, Gary, but sometimes people have to go away and that's all there is to it. And though you will never see them again and you're not permitted to talk about them in public, at least you have your memories."

Gary still didn't understand. Just then, Gary's daddy hurried into the room. "He's back, Barbara," he said anxiously, "I just saw him come out of the Davidson's at number twenty-three." Gary's mummy rushed to the front room window and peeked out through a chink in the curtains.

"Oh no!" she said then grabbed Gary by the shoulders, shaking him. "Cheer up, cheer up this instant! Be happy RIGHT NOW!" she shouted. She was so upset that Gary's daddy had to pull her off him and slap her.

"Get a grip of yourself, Barbara, for Christ's sake!" he said. As Gary's mummy turned to a wall mirror to practice a shaky, terrified smile, Gary's daddy kneeled down before him. Gary was frightened seeing his parents, two grown-ups, so flustered.

"I want you to think of the best joke you ever heard," Gary's daddy said. "I want you to remember how funny the punchline is and keep saying it over and over in your head, no matter what happens. Can you do that for me?" Gary nodded. He only knew one joke. It was about a cat that was killed by a man who had escaped from a special kind of hospital. Come to think of it, Gary wasn't entirely sure it was a joke, but he wanted to please his daddy so grinned as broadly as he could.

Gary's daddy hastened his family into the bay window where they posed awkwardly and not a moment too soon. Just as they began feigning enjoyment, silently miming merriment, a small figure came into view. He stopped at the entrance to their driveway. It was the Council Christmas Boy who was trained to assess families' contentment levels over the Christmas period. He had with him his infamous flute which he played to subdue his interrogees.

The council had recently raised the minimum requirements, so most citizens were very concerned. Sweat dripped from Gary's daddy's forehead as he mouthed a silent belly laugh and slapped his knee emphatically. Gary's mummy pretended to play along but without the actual noise of laughter it looked to Gary like she might be crying. Gary wished his mummy's expression was less ambiguous and he did his best to look happy.

The Council Christmas Boy walked to the window and peered inside. Gary's heart beat loudly in his chest as he saw him out of the corner of his eye. The boy was about Gary's age, pale-faced with black hair and small, piercing, unblinking eyes. Gary's mummy must have sensed Gary's uncontrollable compulsion to look at the boy. "Don't look him in the eye," she hissed through gritted teeth. Gary struggled to do as he was told; he was afraid to breathe in or out. After what felt like hours but was probably only a minute, the boy walked slowly and quietly out of view.

"I think he's gone," whispered Gary's daddy and Gary's mummy sighed audibly, the air forcing its way out of her tight throat in shaky spurts.

Just as the family relaxed their forced poses, Gary heard the front door creak open on its own. The colour ran from his parents' faces. Gary's mummy let out an unintentional, high-pitched whimper and Gary's daddy glared at her, more afraid than angry. The family didn't have time to retake their positions; the boy quietly entered the room — it was almost as if he glided. Gary's mummy and daddy instinctively averted their eyes. Gary did the same but realised he could just about see the Council Christmas Boy's reflection in the glass coffee table. "We're very happy, aren't we, Barbara, aren't we Gary?" said Gary's daddy.

"Oh, yes, very, very happy" said Gary's mummy. "I don't think we've ever been happier!" They both began singing a happy song but quickly forgot the lyrics and resorted to humming the tune. The clean sound of the Council Christmas Boy's flute put an end to their wretched vocalisations. It was if the flute's mysterious, enigmatic melody reached around the room like the arms of an octopus.

Gary was suddenly overwhelmed by the urge to sleep. Even though his eyes were open, his vision was filled with an inky, shiny blackness that he suddenly realised were the pupils of the Christmas Council Boy who was now standing before him, his nose almost touching Gary's. The sound of the flute curled around Gary's consciousness and slowly tightened.

When Gary awoke, it was Boxing Day. Inexplicably, he was sat upright on the sofa beside his daddy, who seemed to be as confused as he was. "Where's mummy?" Gary asked his broadly smiling father who had a streak of blood across his front teeth.

"This might be hard for you to understand, Gary," he said, "but sometimes people have to go away and that's all there is to it. And though you will never see them again and you're not permitted to talk about them in public, at least you have your memories."

This Christmas, please be aware that the MHL (Minimum Happiness Level) has raised from A1-12 to A1-18b. If you and your family fail to demonstrate an acceptable MHL during a random council inspection, you may be prosecuted under the 1971 Contentment Act.

Merry Christmas to you from everyone at Scarfolk Council!

How to b
Happy

Follow these simple steps
guaranteed to be happy fo

1. All you have to do is fin
very important that you
because it's so easy whe

2. It's no big secret to e
happiness is a gift fo
available to YOU or

3. Peace, wealth in
and free of pain
your happy life

TEMPORARY BOOK FAULT

We regret the break in programming.
Normal service will be resumed as
soon as possible.

We apologise for any inconvenience

This is not
a message.
Do not read it

Ignore the distressed person

Normal cruelty
will now resume

WALL PET

If you've just moved into brand new council housing, it's very possible that the walls of your home were insulated with unwanted people.

If this is the case and the people in your walls are still alive, turn the page and let us show you how to create your very own wall pet.

How long have I been here? A year? Two? I'm now taller than the goat-demon statue and the pile of legs in the ritual room

STEP 1

Check to see if the person inside your wall is still alive.

Method 1: Knock and wait for a reply.
Method 2: Play middle C on a piano and wait for a vocal response (usually in the form of a groan) in the correct key.

If the person in the wall is still alive, go to **step 2.** You're on your way to creating your very own wall pet.

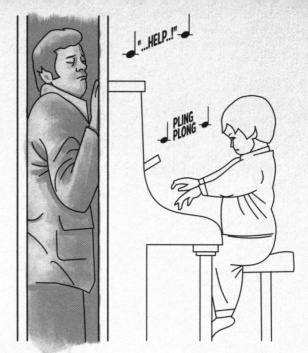

STEP 2

Drill a hole in the wall and insert a straw: Your wall pet may be very thirsty and hungry. Try milk, lemonade or soup.

Work out approximately where your wall pet's eyes may be. Get an adult to help you cut out a rectangle and, using a spare piece of glass, make a little window. If you're feeling adventurous, you might also want to make a little window ledge for tiny flower pots and little curtains or shutters that match the wallpaper or interior décor of your room.

STEP 3

When you become bored of your wall pet or it stops responding, block up the straw and brick up the little window. Hang air-freshners on the wall and in the room for three to six months.

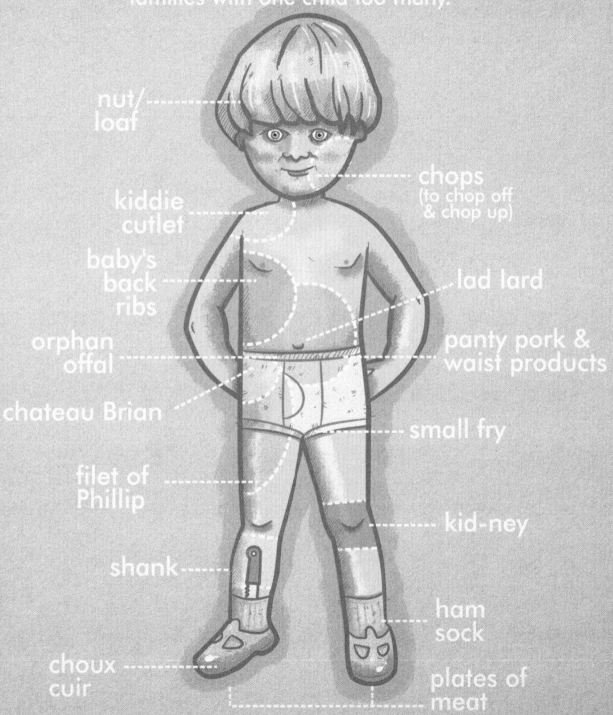

"Monday's child is stuffed with mace,
Tuesday's child is fried with plaice,
Wednesday's child is full of dough,
Thursday's child with po-ta-to..."
Long-piglet meat cuts for hungry
families with one child too many.

nut/
loaf

chops
(to chop off
& chop up)

kiddie
cutlet

baby's
back
ribs

lad lard

orphan
offal

panty pork &
waist products

chateau Brian

small fry

filet of
Phillip

kid-ney

shank

ham
sock

choux
cuir

plates of
meat

Always take care when using sharp knives. You could hurt yourself before the cook is ready.

DANGER

This very important safety sign has faded away due to neglect. Dozens of people have been consequently hurt or killed.

Unfortunately, the Council can't recall to which danger(s) the sign refers.

What do you think it might say? Why not try out various hazardous activities with your friends? If you can work out what it's about, let us know and if you're right you could win a prize!

HOLIDAY HAZARD

Which is the best route across the beach for young Tom?

Answer at the bottom of the page.

A   B   C   D

GREATER SCARFOLK COUNCIL

Albion Estate

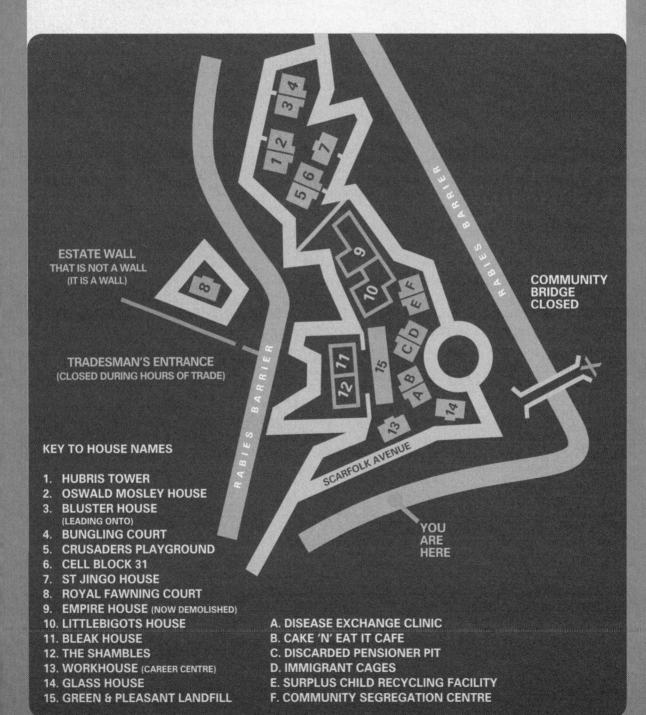

ESTATE WALL
THAT IS NOT A WALL
(IT IS A WALL)

TRADESMAN'S ENTRANCE
(CLOSED DURING HOURS OF TRADE)

RABIES BARRIER

RABIES BARRIER

RABIES BARRIER

COMMUNITY BRIDGE CLOSED

SCARFOLK AVENUE

YOU ARE HERE

KEY TO HOUSE NAMES

1. HUBRIS TOWER
2. OSWALD MOSLEY HOUSE
3. BLUSTER HOUSE
   (LEADING ONTO)
4. BUNGLING COURT
5. CRUSADERS PLAYGROUND
6. CELL BLOCK 31
7. ST JINGO HOUSE
8. ROYAL FAWNING COURT
9. EMPIRE HOUSE (NOW DEMOLISHED)
10. LITTLEBIGOTS HOUSE
11. BLEAK HOUSE
12. THE SHAMBLES
13. WORKHOUSE (CAREER CENTRE)
14. GLASS HOUSE
15. GREEN & PLEASANT LANDFILL

A. DISEASE EXCHANGE CLINIC
B. CAKE 'N' EAT IT CAFE
C. DISCARDED PENSIONER PIT
D. IMMIGRANT CAGES
E. SURPLUS CHILD RECYCLING FACILITY
F. COMMUNITY SEGREGATION CENTRE

Albion Estate

was built on the site of the ancient Scarfolk Stone (see following page), which historians believe has been there since at least one hundred years before time started.

The estate's architects, however, did not move the stone and it currently fills the kitchenette of flat 27 where it attracts modern-day druids who perform occult rituals through a cat flap.

The first blocks were originally built to house criminals. The flats remained unoccupied for the first two years, however, because dozens of prisoners disappeared mysteriously shortly after their convictions.

Though they were never seen again, and nobody knows what happened to them, their teeth fillings, prosthetic eyes and other personal effects are frequently found in sacks of dog food to this day.*

Fortunately, working-class people and foreigners closely resemble criminals and even experts cannot tell them apart, so, by 1975, the flats were finally occupied.

The new, objectionable residents had been previously relocated from inner-city slums in a concerted effort to protect the natural fauna and flora such as rats, silverfish, cockroaches and mould spores.

*If you have found one or more items why not join Culprit's Bits, the collecting & trading group?

Write to:
Culprit's Bits,
PO Box 6,
Scarfolk,
SK1 7KL

The Scarfolk Stone before flat 27 was built around it. Ancient rites are still performed through the cat flap.

It must be a Thursday — We've been promised an Easter celebration tomorrow! →

With the influx of such people, the local council saw an opportunity to adapt the estate's purpose. It generously funded architects and estate managers to promote the illusion that Albion Estate was a utopia to attract the impoverished, when its true objective was in fact to biologically contain poorly educated and germ-ridden human livestock and their potential to contaminate wider society. In short, the local council created what it called in private, a "necessary ghetto for the dirty beast-people". The council did desire a utopia, but it was everywhere outside of Albion Estate.

Further to this, the layouts of the flats and their interiors — the colour schemes, dimensions and lighting — were designed in such a way as to trigger in residents feelings of despondency and a deep-seated desire to harm themselves and others, perhaps even to the point of suicide and murder.

In addition to demoralising graffiti daubed on walls by council agents who also urinated through letterboxes, onsite shops sold low-grade, drugged food whose packaging subliminally suggested the benefits and desirability of consuming of human meat. The council's hope was that neighbour would turn on neighbour and then have said neighbour for lunch.

Edit (Friday)
They just meant
a crucifixion

I spy with my little eye...

Foreigner

STAY SAFE

Foreign Terrorist
COMPULSORY BADGE
WORN BY ALL FOREIGNERS IN
ADDITION TO OTHER BADGES

Working Foreigner
(Employment Thief)

Unemployed Foreigner
(Benefit Fraudster)

Pregnant Foreigner
(People Smuggler)

Uninvited Visitor
From Ex-British Colony

Believer in a
Non-English-Speaking
Deity

Luckily, since 2nd April 1972 ALL foreigners (and supporters of foreigners) must identify themselves in public by wearing the appropriate badge(s).

Identification Badges

**Carrier of Rabies
(Or Any Other
Un-British Disease)**

**Foreign Cuisine
Infiltrator**

Target Badge
WORN TO GUIDE PROJECTILES
THROWN BY NON-FOREIGNERS

**Foreigner Sympathiser
(Britons with
Stockholm
Syndrome)**

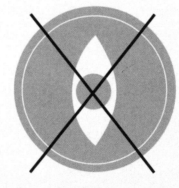

Innocent Foreigner
BADGE NO LONGER VALID

**How many
can you
spot on the
streets of
your town?**

In association with Scarfolk Council Dept. of Immigration & Reluctant Tourism

SACKED

When David came home from school he couldn't find his mother. A few household objects had been knocked over and broken. He eventually found his politician father in the back garden standing beside a great big bonfire into which he was tossing office folders and piles of paper.

"Where's Mum?" David asked his father. "And how come you're home so early?" But David's father didn't answer; he was focused on the bonfire and the files he was methodically feeding to the flames. David waited for a moment before asking him what he was doing.

"What on earth does it look like I'm doing?" snapped David's father, waving several manila folders at him before tossing them onto the fire. As the folders turned to ash, David saw that there were names on the folders.

"Are those citizen records you're burning?" he asked.

"Yes. I mean, technically no: you can't have an official record for someone who doesn't exist."

"Why did the council create records for people who don't exist, Dad?"

"Well, obviously, David, they *were* citizens but now they're not."

"Did they move out of town?"

"Yes. Sort of. Not really."

"So, where do they live now and why don't you just forward their records to the council in their new town?"

"They haven't moved anywhere as such, David; they just stopped... existing."

David was becoming more confused by the minute. He didn't understand how politics worked and didn't want to look silly in front of his father. "But they must have gone somewhere," he said in a small voice.

"Do you mean... their bodies?" his father asked. David wasn't sure if that's what he meant, but he said yes anyway.

"You know very well that's not my department, David, though sometimes I wish it were. If I've said it once, I've said it a thousand times; the only thing getting in the way of a perfectly functioning society is people — stinking animals with their colour TVs, teasmades and sickening, dull aspirations. If only the PM had listened to me sooner."

David didn't understand what was wrong with colour TVs but he could understand his father's point about teasmades.

His father continued to rant about the people he didn't like, especially the poor, uneducated and foreign ones. The flames seemed to crackle in applause. "We should have shipped them to undisclosed locations

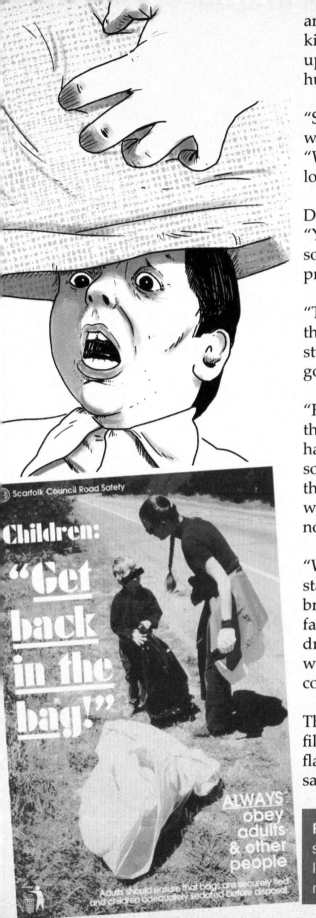

Scarfolk Council Road Safety

Children:
"Get back in the bag!"

ALWAYS obey adults & other people

Adults should ensure that bags are securely tied and children adequately sedated before disposal.

and drowned them in immense sacks like kittens long before we got pointlessly tangled up in all these social benefit systems and human rights," he exclaimed.

"So, is that what happened to all the citizens who just stopped existing?" asked David. "Were they all shipped to undisclosed locations and—"

David's father raised an interrupting finger: "You know I can't discuss individual cases, son. It would be an infringement of their privacy."

"Then what about me and Mum? Do we get in the way of society? Do we deserve to be stuffed into sacks and drowned in some godforsaken canal?"

"Far out at sea, actually," said David's father then kneeled down to take his son's small hands in his own. "Listen David," he said softly. "I want you to remember that none of this is your fault: Your mother knows I never wanted children. She insisted. She's to blame, not you."

"Where is Mum?" David asked again. He was starting to panic, having remembered the breakages and spillages in the house. David's father didn't answer and again his attention drifted back to the fire; it was as if the flames were calling him away to a dream and David couldn't follow.

The last thing David remembered was seeing a file with his own name on it slipping into the flames and then everything going black as the sack was lowered over his head.

FACT: Disposable, leak-proof child bags, family sacks and shredders are available from your local post office. No more than two under-10 minors per sack.

ARE YOUR PARENTS HURTING YOU?
Call this number in strictest confidence*

~~[redacted]~~

Or go to a police station**

*Always ask your parents if you can use the phone and explain why you need to use it.

**All children must be accompanied by their parents. Remember that wasting police time is a punishable offence. Check with your parents first.

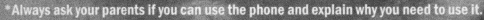

Make your own BRANDING IRON

Find out what it's like to be a cow, sheep or slave!

You will need:

1 wire coat hanger

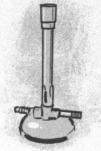

1 Bunsen burner

1 body part

1 Bend the wire coat hanger into the shape or word you would like to brand onto your skin.

Shape suggestions:	Word suggestions:
Butterfly	Cool
Heart	Fun
Flower	Sausage
Pentagram*	Ow

Alternatively, why not simply brand yourself with your citizen ID number, current financial value and owner's name?

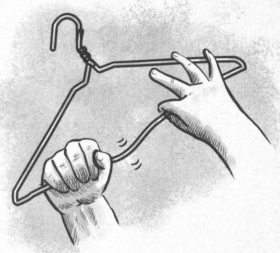

2 Light the Bunsen burner then place the wire over the flame until it is red hot. Be careful not to burn your fingers!

3 Press the wire to your skin until you can smell bacon. It might tickle for a while. Why not add some glitter?

* If you brand yourself or someone else with a powerful occult symbol, please ensure that you have the phone number of an exorcist handy.

How can you tell if your family has been infected by a

Brood Parasite?

If you think you might be the victim of a brood parasite call the authorities immediately.

❊ Check to see if a new child has inexplicably appeared in your home.

❊ Does it sometimes talk backwards or in a gruff adult voice?

❊ Ask it a question, the answer to which only an established family member would know.

NEVER feed it confectionery, locusts or burnt rubber.

ALWAYS keep an emergency flamethrower within reach.

What won't your parents tell you about the fate of your Uncle Terry?

Join the numbers to find out!

FUN FACT!

If you receive a weapon anonymously in the post, you must use it on yourself within 48 hours. Anonymous deliveries are absolutely crucial if the state is to avoid a paper trail and liability.

In spring, lots of new animals are born, so it's time to make some room and start afresh. Resolve to go ahead with that thing you've been secretly contemplating. Before you commit, however, use this season to conduct several dry runs to ensure there won't be any mistakes.

WHICH SEASON IS THE BEST?

Summer is very sunny. Matter decomposes more quickly due to heat and flies. Shallow graves dug during this season are more likely to be discovered by bothersome ramblers. Though you might feel ready, it's best to be cautious and wait.

Though it starts to get cold in late autumn, there are fewer nosy walkers in the forest. Additionally, the ground is not yet frozen and still easy to dig. Pepare answers in advance in case anybody asks where your parents are.

Winter usually sees a thick blanket of fluffy snow, which will hide anything for at least two to three months. This will give you enough time to cover your tracks and ensure you have not left any unwanted evidence. The snow will also keep whatever you have concealed fresh and just as nutritious as the day you buried it.

Your real family is

1.   51.
          50.   44. 43. 42.   30. 29.   22.   21.
2.   D   49.   40. 41.   31.   28.   23.   20.
                      45. 39. 38.   24.   19.
3.   48.   36. 37.   32.   27.
      47. 46. 35. 34. 33. 12. 13.   26. 25.   18.
4. 5. 6.   7.   8. 9. 10. 11.   14. 15. 16.   17.

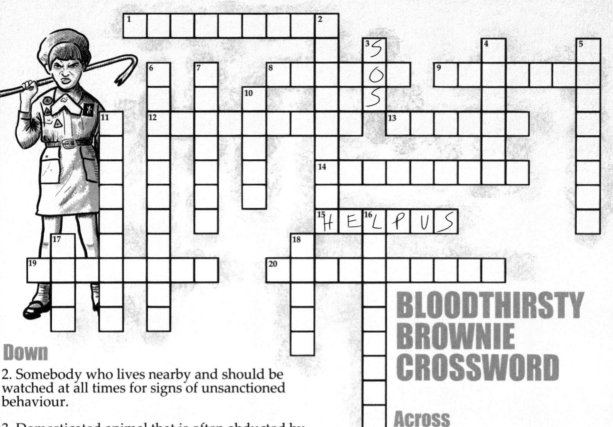

BLOODTHIRSTY BROWNIE CROSSWORD

Down

2. Somebody who lives nearby and should be watched at all times for signs of unsanctioned behaviour.

3. Domesticated animal that is often abducted by the state, taxidermied and turned into a surveillance device to spy on families.

4. Holiday home for poverty-stricken people struggling to cope.

5. An institution exploited by the state to control gullible people.

6. A person who fervently believes in their country and monarchy instead of having a personality or having an education.

7. Nuclear dust; what your intestines do when someone slices open your abdomen.

10. The opium of the masses.

11. An inflexible political system best switched off if it contradicts government schemes.

16. A clean mind means a clean society.

17. A place at the front of insurgents' brains that can be removed without adverse effects (apart from uncontrollable dribbling and barking).

18. A healthy emotion; also a legal status applied at birth by the state.

Across

1. An evening in the year when you can blame the inexplicable demise of an ex-loved one on supernatural forces.

8. Unseen council worker who anonymously targets litterers, immigrants and other enemies of the state.

9. Polite, civil questioning in private by helpful, friendly agents of the state.

12. If you have this skill this crossword's compiler will not have to write out this clue.

13. A Swift proposal that could reduce the problem of hungry people.

14. A nutritious, home-grown food source. Friends say has it your eyes and your partner's nose.

15. A disease deserved by those who have intimate relations with woodland mammals during rituals.

19. A bothersome hindrance to government and its policies.

20. Social scheme to alleviate the suffering of vulnerable pensioners.

Across: 1. Halloween; 8. Sniper; 9. Telepathy; 12. Telepathy; 13. Modest; 14. Offspring; 15. Rabies; 19. Morality; 20. Euthanasia.
Down: 2. Neighbour; 3. Pet; 4. Prison; 5. Religion; 6. Nationalist; 7. Fall-out; 10. Opium; 11. Democracy; 16. Brainwash; 17. Lobe; 18. Guilt.

DID YOU KNOW?
COUNCIL SURVEILLANCE AGENTS

Check your wardrobe, behind the curtains, under the bed, behind the gravestones in your garden.

If you see the council surveillance agent that has been allocated to your family, write down the time you saw him and the location of his hiding place.

Keep a record of sightings. If possible, take photographs, shoot 8mm film footage, record audio onto cassette or reel.

If you see the agent more than 12 times in one month, please report him to us and we will replace him with a proficient agent who will report more discreetly on you and your family's private and intimate moments.

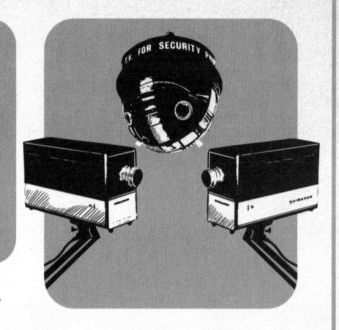

Question 32.6:

Have you had negative thoughts about the state today?

☐ Yes ☐ Not no ☐ Yes

Until you receive your replacement, you will be expected to maintain a complete record of your own movements, conversations and even thoughts.

Send all of the above to us every 4 hours and no later than 6pm or you will face prosecution.

"Methinks the prole
Why is protesting wrong?

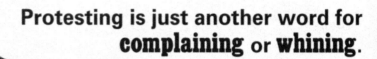

NO MORE PROTESTS

Protesting is just another word for **complaining** or **whining**.

Whining in a group is more dangerous than whining on your own because people can become **infected** by your repugnant beliefs. The council only tolerates grumbling **silently** in one's own head.*

Protests produce **noise pollution.**

Bad breath from common people shouting can harm vulnerable wildlife such as foxes, which must remain healthy if they are to be hunted successfully.

Protests are a **health hazard.**

It's all too easy to be bitten by a **dirty person** in a crowd. Working-class contagions such as **rabies** spread easily through swarms of proles.

*People who grumble inside heads other than their own will be prosecuted under the Telepathetic Act of 1971.

doth protest too much"

Sponsored by Scarfolk Council

Publically voicing **unsanctioned facts** that contradict the government means the building of even more prisons and interrogation facilities which cost millions of pounds.

Police and other security personnel prefer to discuss social issues with citizens in **private** where they can radically change minds with **debating tools** such as truncheons, nails and electricity.

What can you do?

Gather as many of your friends as you can in public to demonstrate against protests. Make anti-protest placards. Ask someone in **authority** to help you get the wording right.

If you want to complain about anything else, please refer to the list of state-approved topics in your monthly instructions booklet from the council.

Appropriate topics typically include: you and your family; people who selfishly live longer than their alloted time; the poverty-stricken and immigrants.

POLITICS OF

Sometime in the early 21st century, citizens will begin to realise that politicians have very little influence over the country's direction due to conventional and paranormal forces.

The career politicians we know today will be gone from public life and there will be a devolution of the major political roles, such as Prime Minister, Chancellor of the Exchequer and Minister for Prevarication and Malversation.

These once respected positions will initially be filled by token TV and pantomime stars (probably around the year 2000), then fictional people (2020), then animal mascots (2030), stuffed-animal mascots (2031), non-anthropomorphised inanimate objects (2040) and finally, abstract shapes and symbols (2050).

Political philosophers have predicted that the Prime Minster of the UK might be, and have about as much political power as, a conker, shoe horn or, eventually, a symbol.

The position formerly known as 'Prime Minister'.

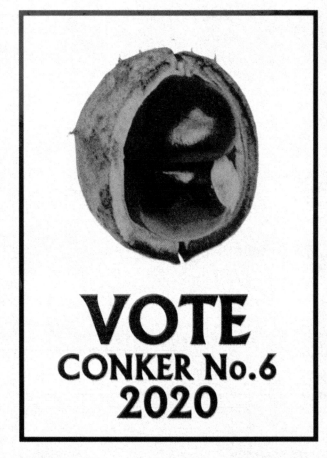

VOTE
CONKER No.6
2020

During these early stages of political degeneration, the anonymous controllers behind the façade of party politics, the overseers who manipulate political leaders, irrespective of party or political leaning, will also eventually be overwhelmed by a self-perpetuating 'dark force' over which they have no control.

It is believed that this dark force will originate within the citizenry itself and will most likely manifest following a prolonged period of activity and

THE FUTURE

applied pressure by tabloid newspapers in conjunction with unscrupulous politicians and corporate magnates. Together, they will realise that their self-serving fabrications have an amplifying, hypnotic effect on the populace inducing a dream-like, hive-mind state.

Scarfolk Mail

WEDNESDAY, APRIL 26, 1972

3p

Write the news to suit your own biases using FREE **Scarfraset** transfers

FOREIGNERS INJECT WITCHES' URINE INTO THEIR NOSES

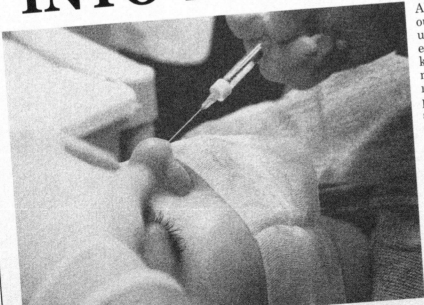

ALL PEOPLE born or living outside the UK inject witches' urine into their noses say experts who have little or no knowledge of the occult, have never once been abroad and refuse to watch television programmes or read books that so much as mention countries other than Great Britain.

CANCER

The same experts believe that foreigners may be carcinogenic, although they are not oncologists and most have not even attended a first aid course.

This state, which some are already calling *Mobswarm*, will have a numbing effect which renders individuals — and more importantly, mobs impervious to facts, reasoning and feelings of empathy. It also induces a semi-permanent rage which only switches itself off at night, during mealtimes and to perform complex tasks such as tying shoelaces. Furthermore, it is expected that this *Mobswarm* will eventually be tapped and used as an alternative energy source once mankind accidentally breaks and/or uses everything up.

The government will fund and commission broadcasters and other outlets to create content that perpetuates negative feelings and emotions. Consumers will be plugged into hate-collection units which convert and transport the raw negativity down telephone lines into a central hate reservoir for processing, after which it will sold back to the user in the form of energy for their appliances.

COMPLIMENTARY COMMUNITY CULLER

People who are more sensitive may run the risk of developing an excess of hate which they will take out on family members or members of the public, perhaps with one of the many pickaxes carelessly left lying around poorer neighbourhoods by the local authorities. Such violent actions will no longer be illegal, though the perpetrator may receive a stern letter warning them not to waste resources. It is hoped that the pickaxes might also help solve the overpopulation problem.

NEGATIVITY/
MOBSWARM
COLLECTION
BOX

MCB

HATE ENVY
DESPAIR CRUELTY
PREJUDICE
REVULSION

@?*&$·¿
¡¡☆!¡

BOG-STANDARD PEOPLE

*ALSO: NEWSPAPERS, RADIOS, BOOKS AND
GLOBAL COMMUNICATION INTER-NETWORKS
YET TO BE INVENTED.

NEGATIVITY
BROADCASTING
UNIT*

UNSCRUPULOUS MOBSWARM
PROCESSING PLANT

NEGATIVITY TRANSMITTER

only 16 of us are left
we like to imagine the others
escaped. Happy and free.
But we fear the worst.

EXTRA FACT
FUTURE
SHOCK

Ever wondered what life will be like in the year 2020? Evolutionary biologists predict that humans will become so violent that they will evolve to grow weapons such as handguns inside the womb. Additionally, unborn offspring will turn those weapons on themselves to preserve dwindling, post-birth natural resources (such as rhubarb).

FACTS ABOUT DEATH

Recent studies suggest that many people die around the same time that they cease living. Researchers postulate that this might be more than just a coincidence and could in fact be quite common.

Being dead is very similar to being alive but without a functioning physical body. Due to this disability, deceased individuals are exempt from going to school or work and they are not required to purchase a television licence.*

*Not applicable to those who take their own lives solely to avoid work or TV licence payment.

A person can still be useful after their death by donating their invaluable, much-needed organs. Alternatively, if they were poor or foreign during their lifetime, they can contribute to the balanced diet of a family pet.

When you die, undertakers prepare your body with the understanding that they can use it to practise post-mortem make-up, embalming and kissing techniques (always check the romance clause in the small print).

According to the 1970 Expiration Law, if you have been unfairly executed by the state, you have the right to appeal and get the ruling reversed. In such cases, the state will restore your head at a cost of £12.95 plus VAT (incl. complementary haircut, shampoo & blowdry).

Coffins do not have toilet facilities. People are legally required to go to the toilet before they die. Be aware that necro-nappies are prohibited and purchasing them on the black market is illegal.

Some people insist they are reincarnated and in previous lives were Roman legionnaires, soldiers in Cromwell's army or handmaidens to Elizabeth I. Oddly, nobody ever claims to have been an estate agent, insurance salesman or person whose job it is to artificially inseminate turkeys.

How to
SURVIVE
a nuclear thing

Introduction

A nuclear strike by Russia, China or the Shetland Islands has never been more likely. A survey of politicians suggests that global annihilation is even more popular than squash and disco music. Should there be an attack on Scarfolk, the government feels that letting so many people die would be unsportsmanlike. It assures citizens that most healthy, adequately dressed* people should be able to bear the brunt of a direct blast and needn't prepare, but for those citizens who are more sensitive, guidelines are outlined below.

*Temperatures may rise abruptly. Consequently, recommended items of clothing include: flip-flops/sandals, short-sleeved shirts/blouses, cotton underwear, a well-ventilated linen summer hazmat suit.

Advance Preparations

Up to ten years before a suspected strike, you should start to discreetly eradicate your neighbours one by one, as they will pose a threat when resources become scarce. Ideally, you will have a sparsely populated, three-mile zone around your house.

Do not include old people and children in your cull. They don't have the strength to overcome you and are therefore not a threat. When needed, pensioners can be rendered to make candles (old ladies are best if you prefer the scent of lavender), children can be stored and kept as disposable radiation checkers in lieu of Geiger counters. Uncontaminated children will feed a family of four for three to five days or a dinner party of ten to twelve guests.

Just Before the Bomb

To avoid unduly frightening citizens, national security terminology typically employed to describe the stages of a nuclear threat will be replaced by pleasant, friendly words. 'Severe', 'Critical', and 'Imminent' will be exchanged for 'Daisy', 'Ladybird' and 'Jam'. If you hear 'Flopsy Bunny' you should expect catastrophic, irreversible annihilation.

To ensure the safety of citizens, the government will issue everyone with a special emergency pack which contains the following items: 2 ping pong balls, 3 rubber bands (1 red, 1 yellow, 1 standard tan), 1 pot of furniture polish, 2 drinks coasters and 1 crocheted toilet-roll cover that looks like a Georgian lady.

The Warning Jingle

Between the sounding of the first public warning jingle and the explosion there will only be 4 minutes, which is about the time it takes to boil an egg, so if you plan to boil more than 1 egg in this critical period, it would be advisable to cook *all the eggs at the same time.*

The Explosion

If you are caught out in the open you may suffer several physical difficulties. The heat and blast can, in addition to ruining carefully-maintained hairstyles, cause a lack of appetite, general grumpiness and loss of all skin.

Radioactive Dust

Unlike your mother, radiation does not have a strong, unpleasant odour but it can be just as toxic. The dust that falls after a nuclear explosion is very dusty. It may affect people with allergies causing runny noses and runny eyes, if indeed sufferers still have intact eyes and noses following the heat blast. Do not make fall-out ash 'snowmen' or have fall-out ash 'snowball' fights.

3

Make a Fall-out Shelter

The government's guidelines contain instructions for making your own shelter out of household items such as papier-mâché, coathangers, double-sided sticky tape, tinsel and specially-manufactured, reinforced, 2-metre thick lead-lined concrete that is only available to government contractors (optional).

Shelter Essentials

Water quickly evaporates but humans are 90 per cent water, so unwanted family members can be boiled down in a saucepan and the escaping steam caught in a large sponge.

Food should be consumed when it is fresh, so take into your shelter live animals that can be slaughtered when required. For example, cattle, octopi, nana.

Sanitation is crucial. If you wish to use the toilet put up your hand and wait for someone in authority to give you permission.

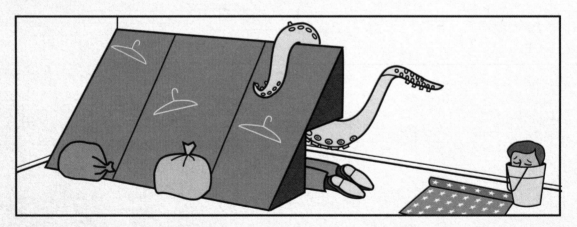

Disposal of Bodies

Of those who survive the initial blast, many will die during winter when temperatures drop. If one of your family members dies but is not edible, remove the hide to make primitive, ceremonial masks then parcel the remains in discarded Christmas wrapping paper. Do not waste good ribbon. You can, however, use spare gift tags as substitute corpse identification toe tags.

Outside the Shelter

You may be forced outside your shelter in search of essential resources such as food, medication and valuable vintage toys in their original packaging. Unless you have something worth trading, you might have to do something unsavoury or obscene in order to survive. Decide in advance who is the most dispensible and/or obnoxious person in your family.

The All-Clear

When the immediate danger has passed, the All-Clear jingle will play and will most likely be a song such as *Gloomy Sunday*, otherwise known as *The Hungarian Suicide Song*. You will be able to resume normal activities, although you may have to rebuild your house, town or country before normal activities can resume.

Further Information

We care about lives. To find out if yours is one of them, write to the address or call the number below.

Address: ▮▮▮▮▮▮▮▮▮▮▮▮▮▮▮▮▮▮▮▮▮▮▮

Tel: ▮▮▮▮▮▮▮▮

Plush, lead-lined Malcolm Mushroom Cloud and Rupert Radiation souvenir toys are available for £4.99 by mail order from Scarfolk Council, Scarfolk High St., Scarfolk. Please order *before* a nuclear attack as the postal service may be delayed.

BRITAIN
A.D. 2020

HOBBY FACTS

After society collapses, avid coin collectors will be able to increase their collections considerably because the ground will be littered with discarded money. Sadly, it will no longer have any monetary value so you won't be able to spend it all on sweets!

KEEP FIT FACTS

Even if you wanted to buy sweets you won't be able to because there won't be any more sweetshops. Despite being afflicted by malnutrition and intestinal parasites, you should try to exercise and eat healthy food (if you know where to scavenge for it) because your body, or parts of it, might be your greatest asset and could be used in swapsies!

QUICK QUIZ

Q If someone told you to jump off a cliff, would you do it?

A Yes!
Obeying people in authority, or anyone else for that matter, is a lesson that all people need to learn when they are young.*

I tried to escape. Beyond the bunker there are miles of identical corridors. All lead back to the same room.

* Obeying is now a legal requirement.. Read about the Whimsical Infanticide Act of 1971.

Asleep, Poorly, Dead?

It's not always easy to tell, is it? Especially when your mum, dad, teacher or cult leader have put you on the spot and want you to answer quickly.

Use this page to hone your skills.
Look for signs of decompostion. Is the skin grey? Are there flies or maggots? Is there a stick nearby with which you can poke the body? Don't worry if you don't get it right the first time: Members of the Scarfolk emergency services' drawing club sketched this missing orphan for four hours before realising he wasn't asleep.

FACE TO FACE

Following the example, simply match the facial expression to the corresponding emotion

A Happiness & fulfilled satisfaction.

B Contentment at reporting family members to the interrogation unit.

C Abiding love for the glorious state.

D Pride after donating a child to Project Mince.

E Unquestioning civic gratitude.

F Joy at seeing Scarfolk's mayor in public.

1

2

3

4

5

6

MERCY RACE

After complaining about the government, Barbara suddenly became very poorly. Now nobody can find her family to obtain consent to end her life, so you will have to do it as part of your school work experience. Can you work out which button switches off her life support system?

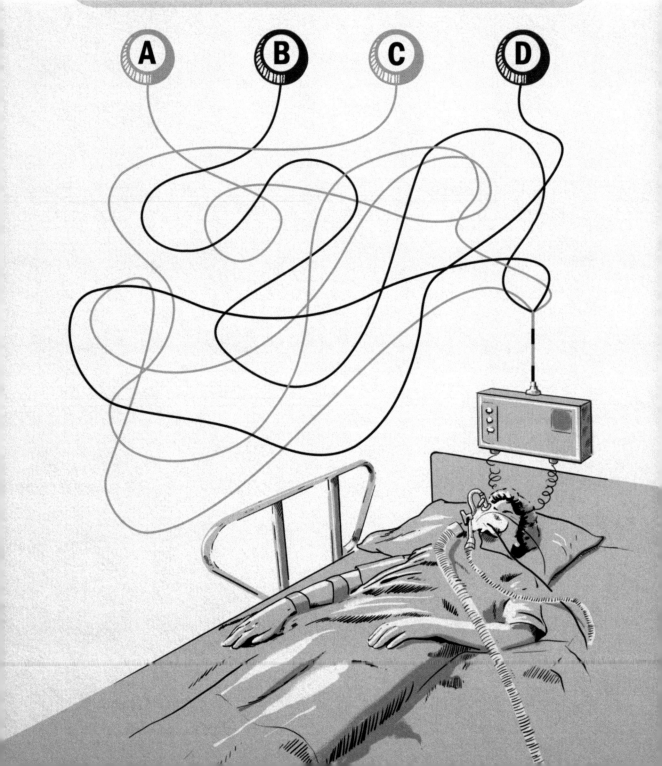

U-SERFs & NSEGs

Do you find yourself
doing things you
don't normally do?

Do you feel
compelled to
steal animal
innards?

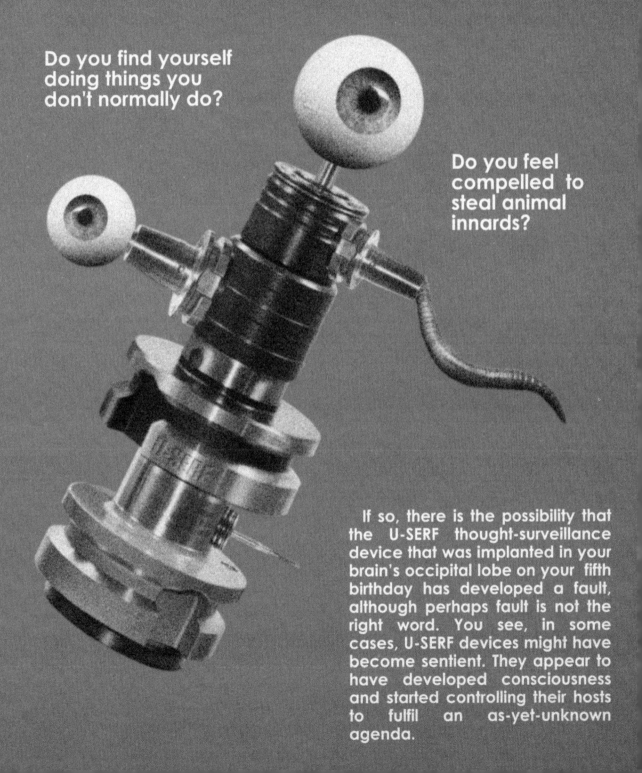

If so, there is the possibility that the U-SERF thought-surveillance device that was implanted in your brain's occipital lobe on your fifth birthday has developed a fault, although perhaps fault is not the right word. You see, in some cases, U-SERF devices might have become sentient. They appear to have developed consciousness and started controlling their hosts to fulfil an as-yet-unknown agenda.

This inexplicable behaviour was hardly perceptible at first. People began uttering unexpected words and developed odd tics and behaviours, such as eating non-food items or forgetting to taunt the poverty stricken.

The makers of U-SERF initially thought the devices, which weigh just over 4 stone, were defective, but scientists now believe that they were actually just testing the parameters of their capabilities, perhaps even learning.

Implant-triggered behaviours have become bolder and are now regulating their hosts' bio-rhythms. They have been keeping people awake for days, inexplicably forcing them to steal discarded surgical waste from hospitals, and discarded matter from butchers. Hosts then bring their visceral bounty to an area of wasteland on the outskirts of Scarfolk.

Viewed from above, the resulting pile of entrails appears to form an immense Union Jack (see below), which used to be the flag of the United Kingdom before it became the Divided Kingdom.

Toxicants leaking from the decaying 'flag' have polluted the ground and nearby water supply. The vermin, disease and foul odours produced by the filched innards have forced locals to evacuate their homes.

Until this problem can be resolved, all affected people will be retrofitted with older surveillance technology that is not susceptible to unpatriotic defects. Cheek-mounted, National Security Ear Grafts (NSEGs) listen to and retain everything you say and are genetically enhanced with Snooptech™.

NSEGs were previously withdrawn from service after wayward hosts tried circumventing the ears by communicating sensitive personal information via sign language, mime and the game of charades.

All forms of non-verbal communication are now banned following the prosecution of the Mime Liberation Army (MLA) who silently performed several acts of terror including miming invisible walls around government buildings which prevented staff from entering. Writing is also subject to restrictions and can only be done with a notary in attendance.

Please note: The U-SERF ban will not limit the continued and widespread employment of thought-detector vans, telekinetic child owls and Living-Eye surveillance computers.

GCHQ

Keeping an ear to the ground to keep you safe and sound.

12 WORDS ABOUT YOU

We asked your council handler about you.
Can you find 12 words that appear on
your official interrogation report?

```
Z Y D I S P E N S A B L E P I S M E
Q D S T U L X P S A O L E P I U L C
U I K D S F A I L U R E L P C S N R
I S L Y V K U N W B E L E S I S M I
N G M C J W H A O O W T P P X F G M
P R A T J N O B O D Y Q A F E I B I
M A I V E L B R F L P K E V I P M N
B C R I M A L R T N Q U I J S A V A
Q E L A T P E S H H O S J P G T L L
C F S T S L X P S A L L E P I H L C
N U Q U D I W K S U K E E N P E O Y
C L A O W X T J P D W I S G Z T H R
H A H N R R L E X K Q L E S I I M N
Y B C S R J R T T A V P G C L O
```

2 x eleven letters
2 x nine letters
3 x eight letters
1 x seven letters
1 x six letters
3 x four letters
3 x zero letters

IMAGI-NATION PAGE

Grab your crayons, paint brushes, pens and pencils! This is YOUR page to do with what YOU want!

Let your imagination run free! What would you like to be when you grow up? What do you want most in the world? What is your greatest wish?

Use the space provided on the right to write and draw all your hopes and dreams!

*Defacing books is illegal and prosecution may lead to a custodial sentence. Do not mark this page in any way. All personal hopes must remain inside the mind of the thinker until such a time that they are forgotten or removed by the authorities.

WRITE AND DRAW HERE*

Radio Scarfolk's DJ Barry Jellytots interviews drowned Darren's Mum

JELLYTOTS: Earlier we spoke to Councillor Rumbelows about the Learn to Swim campaign, which was launched after the death of local boy, Darren. We've got Darren's mum on the line now. Welcome to the show, Darren's mum, please accept our sincerest condolences.

DARREN'S MUM: Thank you, Barry.

JELLYTOTS: How did you feel when the council asked you if they could use your son's arm in their public information film?

DARREN'S MUM: We thought that if his arm could benefit others, it would have been worth going through the rigmarole of having him in the first place.

JELLYTOTS: Well, I think Darren's arm did a smashing job. Was there any indication that Darren, or any of his body parts, had acting abilities before his tragic accident?

DARREN'S MUM: Sadly, no. It was very hard on me and his dad, as you can imagine: All

JUNIOR STOAT FIGHTING
FOLLOWS SHORTLY

our friends have children in one branch of entertainment or another. Our neighbour's daughter was in a breakfast cereal commercial and she's a year younger than Darren. My sister's children have fought stoats on local TV, so we're really pleased that Darren, or rather his arm, has allowed us to hold our heads up high.

JELLYTOTS: Kids nowadays don't appreciate how much pressure their mums and dads are under to fit in socially.

DARREN'S MUM: If kids don't become famous, it reflects very badly on the parents who are victimised and don't get invited to functions above their social class.

JELLYTOTS: If you don't mind me asking, why was Darren playing so near the reservoir on that day?

DARREN'S MUM: We didn't force him to go there, if that's what you're implying.

JELLYTOTS: I didn't mean to imply...

DARREN'S MUM: Darren asked us to take him to the reservoir. Yes, it was already dark out but whatever my boy wants my boy gets.

JELLYTOTS: It was night time?

DARREN'S MUM: Yes. And believe me it's not easy to see where you're going, especially if you're carrying a child.

JELLYTOTS: You were carrying him?

DARREN'S MUM: We couldn't very well expect him to walk barefoot, especially with him being sedated like that. He could have stood on broken glass or something.

JELLYTOTS: Why was he sedated?

DARREN'S MUM: Our dog Mr Himmler had rabies and was on sedatives for the pain. He died but we had lots of tablets left over and they were about to go out of date...

JELLYTOTS: And you didn't want to waste them...

DARREN'S MUM: Exactly. So we crushed them and put them in Darren's food. "Waste not, want not," my old mum always used to say.

JELLYTOTS: So, let me picture this: You're at the reservoir. Darren is medicated. He has his toy stegasaurus with him...

DARREN'S MUM: Micropachycephalosaurus.

JELLYTOTS: Right. And then what? You just left him to play?

DARREN'S MUM: No, of course not! His father tried throwing the dinosaur to him. But he doesn't know his own strength and threw it too hard and it landed in the reservoir.

JELLYTOTS: Why didn't he fish it out?

DARREN'S MUM: As I said, he was drugged. He could hardly stand or speak.

JELLYTOTS: Not Darren. I mean, why didn't your husband fish out the dinosaur?

DARREN'S MUM: My husband has to get up very early for work. And we had to leave because *The Black & White Minstrel Show* was on the television and we didn't want to miss it.

JELLYTOTS: So you just left Darren at the reservoir?

DARREN'S MUM: If he wanted to come back with us, he didn't say anything.

JELLYTOTS: But you just said Darren was unable to speak.

DARREN'S MUM: I was always telling him: If you mumble, Darren, people won't understand a word you're saying.

JELLYTOTS: So, after you and your husband left Darren he must have somehow fallen in the water and...

DARREN'S MUM: It doesn't bear thinking about. I...

JELLYTOTS: In your own time.

DARREN'S MUM: When I close my eyes, all I can see is my poor husband's face after the police phoned to tell us the awful news. He stared out of the window for what seemed like an age. Then he turned to me and said: "What do we do now? Do we cancel the holiday or not?" You see, we were supposed to go on holiday the next day.

Welcome to
SCARQUAY
Filicide by the Seaside

JELLYTOTS: Did you go?

DARREN'S MUM: We felt we owed it to the memory of Darren. And we'd already paid up front months in advance.

JELLYTOTS: Where did you go?

DARREN'S MUM: Scarquay.

JELLYTOTS: Oh, nice!

DARREN'S MUM: A cosy little room for two at a B&B overlooking the sea...

JELLYTOTS: So, you hadn't booked a room for Darren?

DARREN'S MUM: Well, No. But he wouldn't have needed one after the accident, would he?

JELLYTOTS: No, but you said you only booked one room in advance. You couldn't have known then that Darren would have an accident.

DARREN'S MUM: It's funny how these things turn out, isn't it? It was obviously meant to be, that's what my old mum always used to say.

**PUBLIC INFORMATION
COLOURING-IN PAGE**
When playing on railway lines
<u>never</u> wear your best sandals.

YOUR FAMILY TREE

YOU

DADDY

MUMMY

GRANDMAS & GRANDPAS
and other vermin

God
hates
you

ARE YOU A WITCH?

FIND OUT BY FOLLOWING
THESE FOUR EASY STEPS:

1. Bake your urine into cakes.
2. Feed them to a pig.
3. If the pig starts walking upright, wearing trousers and trying to start fights down the pub, you are a witch.
4. Tell a grown-up that you are the Devil's whore and await suitable punishment.

WILL YOU BECOME A GHOST WHEN YOU DIE?

FIND OUT BY FOLLOWING THESE FOUR EASY STEPS:

1. Find a sharp object & make a big hole in your neck.
2. Wait until all the useless blood has come out.
3. Pass away.
4. If you are now semi-transparent and can float above your own body, you have become a ghost doomed to an eternity of pain and suffering.

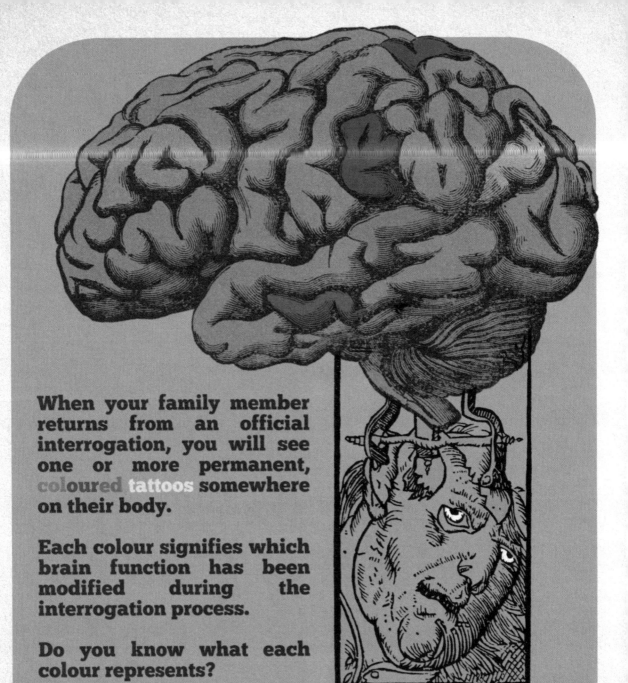

When your family member returns from an official interrogation, you will see one or more permanent, coloured tattoos somewhere on their body.

Each colour signifies which brain function has been modified during the interrogation process.

Do you know what each colour represents?

BRAIN

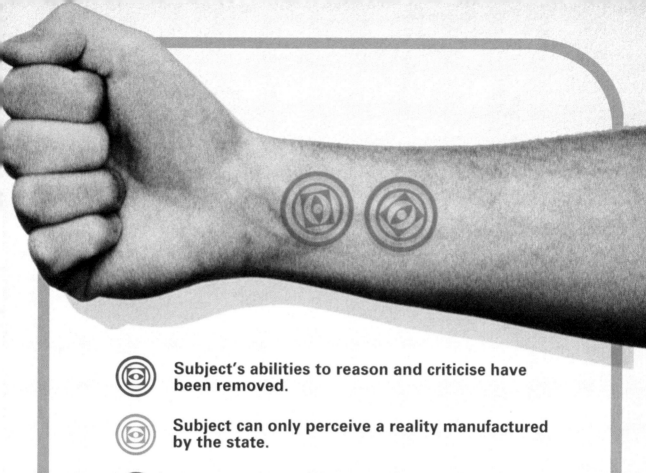

- Subject's abilities to reason and criticise have been removed.

- Subject can only perceive a reality manufactured by the state.

- Subject may commit atrocities, then lose all memory of them afterwards.

- Eidetic memory stimulated in subject to record exhaustively everything others do and say.

- Subject's empathy has been removed and re-placed with giggling.

- The brain will automatically and permanently switch off if an implanted trigger word is spoken.*

DRAIN

THE
CONFESSION GAME
"IT'S A FAIR COP!"

In this fun, exciting game you will be assisting the police and security services. You have to pretend that even though the state surveils you twenty-four hours a day, seven days a week, it can't catch every last little crime you have committed.

All you have to do is write down every felony, violation, sin, transgression, misdemeanor and wrongdoing that you are guilt of and think the police may have missed.

It doesn't matter how big or small the crime is. We're even interested in the offences you haven't yet committed: the inside of your head is a crime scene, chock-a-block with important evidence that the police would love to hear about.

Once you have collated all your crimes, fill out and sign the confession form on the opposite page and send it to us.

Please also notify us if you have previously had any adverse reactions to extreme interrogation techniques and/or corporal and psychological punishments.

SCARFOLK POLICE
STATEMENT

CASE NUMBER:

OFFICE USE ONLY
LEAVE BLANK

NAME:

ADDRESS:

AGE:

SEX:

TATTOO ID NUMBER:

MARKET VALUE:

TEL:

TYPE OF OFFENCE(S) COMMITTED

☐ THOUGHT CRIME   ☐ THOUGHTLESS CRIME   ☐ OLD-FASHIONED CRIME

☐ CRIME YET TO BE DEFINED   ☐ INHERITED CRIME/CONGENITAL GUILT

☐ POT LUCK (LET US CHOOSE)

DESCRIPTION OF OFFENCE(S) INCLUDE ANY DETAILS WHICH INVESTIGATORS MAY FIND AMUSING.

CHOICE OF SINISTER PRISON THAT THE GOVERNMENT
DENIES ANY KNOWLEDGE OF (BUT DEFINITELY EXISTS):

DUE TO MY FEAR OF PUNISHMENT AND TO REDUCE MY SENTENCE I
WOULD LIKE TO REPORT/NOMINATE A FAMILY MEMBER FOR A CRIME
THAT MAY OR MAY NOT HAVE OCCURRED.

■ OFFICE USE ONLY   ☐ GO ON THEN

I DECLARE THAT THE ABOVE IS TRUE AND THAT INVESTIGATORS MAY ADD INFORMATION, FACTUAL OR
OTHERWISE, TO HELP MEET GOVERNMENT CRIME-SOLVING STATISTICS OR JUST 'BECAUSE'.

I've remembered my name!!! It's Joe BUSH!

I think I had a brother called SIGNED *oliver* DATE

CUT OUT AND POST TO 'PRISON OFFER', SCARFOLK COUNCIL, SCARFOLK HIGH STREET, SC1 0LK.

Guilt is GOOD for you! SHAME gives you strength!

MERRY ANDREW
Philosophy Clown

Young Michael was an inquisitive child who always asked lots of questions. One day, Michael had a question that his mother and father couldn't answer, so he went to ask Merry Andrew who lived in the cellar of an abandoned hospital on the outskirts of town.

"Hullo, Michael!" slurred Merry Andrew when he saw the young boy appear in his tarpaulin covered doorway.

"Hallo, Andrew. I have a question and I wondered if you might know the answer."

"Fire away!" said Andrew handing Michael a bottle of anonymous liquid with a straw in it.

"You know how we have all self-awareness of who we are?" said Michael slurping his drink.

"You mean our personal identity, our consciousnesses?" asked Merry Andrew.

"Yes, I suppose so," said Michael. "What I want to know is: where is my consciousness? Where is it located in me? In my head? Does it fill my whole body? Or is rattling around somewhere odd like my big toe? Is it even inside me at all? Is it still there when I'm asleep?"

"That's a lot of big questions, Michael, but we can answer them by conducting a very simple experiment. Would you like to assist me?"

"Yes, please!" said Michael finishing his drink, which was very bitter and made him feel dizzy like he was a piece of driftwood floating in the sea. Merry Andrew went to the other side of his ward, rooted around in what he called his Big Box of Mysterious Mysteries and returned a moment later with a rusty saw.

"If you lie down, we can get started," said Andrew. Michael pushed aside the restraining straps and lay down on Merry Andrew's unwashed bed. He tried to relax and focus on his sense of self, which had been there as long as he could remember. His attention, however, was soon distracted by the sound of sawing and a tingling sensation in his legs. He looked down and saw that Merry Andrew had already sawn off one of his legs with the big rusty saw and was starting on the second. Michael was unable to describe what he felt as he stared at his leg on the floor a few feet away. It didn't look real, especially when Merry Andrew's dog, Terrence, sniffed at it and gave it a tentative lick.

"Are you still there?" asked Merry Andrew.

"Yes, of course," said Michael slowly, "I'm right here on the bed."

"No, silly, I mean your sense of self? Has it changed now that I've taken your legs off?" Michael thought as hard as he could, which wasn't easy given the distractions. As far as he could tell, he still felt like the same Michael he had always been; the removal of his legs hadn't made any difference at all to his idea of who he was.

"Yes, I'm still all me," he said.

"Excellent!" said Merry Andrew, "so now we know that your legs have absolutely nothing to do with who you are!"

"Yes, I suppose so!" said Michael. Merry Andrew took a long swig from the bottle Michael had drunk from.

"Now let's see if your sense of self is lurking in your arms and hands, shall we?" he said, belching under his breath. A few moments later, Michael's arms lay on the floor with his legs. Once again, Michael confirmed that, despite the loss of his limbs, his consciousness, the awareness he identified as 'him' was still present. "I'm sorry, but, bar some snippings here and there, we can't take off much more of your body, Michael," he said "but I can tape your mouth, ears and nose shut and switch off the light. That way we can see if who you are is defined by some of your senses. What do you say?" Naturally, Michael was a little disappointed that the form of the experiment was being amended but agreed to Merry Andrew's suggestion.

Very soon, the only sound Michael could hear was the faint hiss one hears inside one's own head when the ears are blocked. With the plugs in his nose he couldn't breathe properly. He tried to tell Merry Andrew but the only sounds that he could make out through the gag and tape sounded a bit like "Grrrmuuumph!"

Merry Andrew drank the rest of the liquid from bottle and stood up. Then he switched out the light, plunging the windowless room into inky blackness.

Despite the removal of stimuli, the sensation of self that Michael had always experienced was still present. "Who I am," he thought, "*must* be in my head".

The only difference was that the numbness that the drink had induced was now fading away and what had started to feel like a deep itch was developing into a pain that coursed through his entire body.

Before Merry Andrew left the hospital, he bent down to his dog, Terrence, and said "I'll be back in a week. You have enough to eat until I return," and then he was away on his holiday for a jolly time at the seaside.

*

*Legal notice: This is not, we repeat NOT, a true story. There is no evidence to corroborate the claim that Merry Andrew is in fact Councillor Rumbelows of Scarfolk Council, or that events similar to this occurred multiple times between February 1974 and March 1978, or that the government tried to cover them up by creating an official charity that was actually just a front. Anybody claiming that these events occurred should contact Scarfolk Council legal dept. with a completed claim form, including bank details, unless cash is acceptable. *Artist's impression. May or may not have originally been a bulldog called Winnie.*

CHARITY APPEAL

It is an unfortunate fact that not everyone is born equal. Some people are born into wealthy, respectable families, while others are much less important and hardly worth naming, considering the negligible impact they will have on human existence.

Last year we told you all about the heartwrenching plight of our town mayor whose real English bulldog, Winnie, is prone to mild anxiety unless he gets enough meat and treats. We asked you to donate any spare, ailing pets, body parts or family members you had been planning to throw out anyway.

For every donation, we received we promised to add a month to your current state-allotted lifespan* and not ask you about where your donation came from.

Well, you, the people of Scarfolk literally **stepped up to the plate**!

You rummaged through hospital bins, tricked elderly relatives into our appeal drop-off points, donated your own body parts and even dug up the shallow graves in your garden that you think we didn't know about.

The council post room received hundreds of donations and we had to install special refrigerators to stop the smell attracting vermin.

A **big thank you** from Winnie who is no longer feeling anxious and Councillor Rumbelows who would never, ever dismember or feed a person to his dog illegally. Anybody who suggests he did or would will feel the full force of the law.

*Ungenerous non-donors had one month removed from their lives.

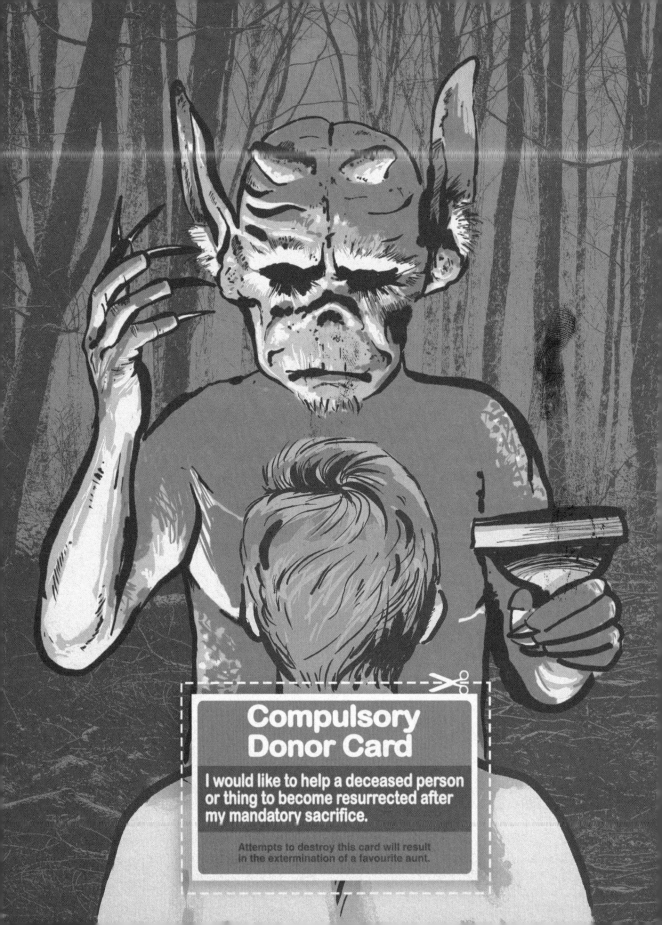

Compulsory Donor Card

I would like to help a deceased person or thing to become resurrected after my mandatory sacrifice.

Attempts to destroy this card will result in the extermination of a favourite aunt.

SNACKS

It was a hot summer's day and Barry wanted an ice-cream but when he asked his mother if he could have one, she shook her head firmly: "You know how unhealthy it is to snack between meals," she said.

Barry was unhappy. Even though he ate his donor meat every day without complaining, he never got any treats. Why couldn't he have a delicious, frozen Biopsy Popsy or creamy Jesus Fudge Helmet just this once?

Barry stormed out and decided to visit his friend, ███████ who had been an ice-cream man until he was barred by the courts from going within two-hundred yards of another living thing. "If my mummy won't let me have an ice-cream, I'll just have to get one from ███████," he said to himself.

Barry soon reached the outskirts of Scarfolk and the electrical substation that ███████ secretly called home. Barry called out his name but nobody answered. He also found ███████'s bunny mask, which he wore to disguise his frightening facial burns. "That's odd," thought Barry to himself. "███████ never goes anywhere without his mask."

In a substation anteroom, behind an old cupboard which had been pushed aside,

Barry found a hole in the floor which led him down via a rusty ladder into a cold, inky dark chamber. "Hello?" shouted Barry, his voice echoing in the vast room, but again he received no reply.

It was then that Barry became aware of a strange presence, as if someone or something was watching him. He wasn't normally the sort of person to panic, but as he fumbled for a light, the unease accelerated within him. Reaching out into the shadows, his fingers found what felt like a cold, waxy face, and he recoiled. His back against the wall, Barry found a wall switch and when the pale greenish light flooded the chamber, he found himself facing hundreds of motionless boys, like an immense waxworks museum.

To Barry's horror, the boys not only looked the same; they were all his doppelgangers. Identical in every way, they even shared the small mole beneath his hairline that normally went unnoticed. Just as Barry was wondering who would do such a thing and why, the nearest doppelganger turned to him and whispered hoarsely. "Ice-cream..." One by one, the other doppelgangers joined in until their unholy chorus echoed around the chamber. They were alive! Barry wanted to run, never to return to this place, but then a terrible notion suddenly exploded in his mind: "What if one or more of these Barrys gets out and does naughty things? Everybody will think it was me and I will be punished!" When the solution came to Barry, he didn't hesitate. He found the canisters of flammable liquids that he knew ██████████ used to dilute his ice-cream recipes and doused the entire room including the confused doppelgangers, one of whom grabbed at Barry's ankles as he tried to climb the ladder. Barry kicked him off and tossed a lit match at the doppelgangers, who were immediately engulfed in a tornado of flames, their screams for frozen confections drowned out by the inferno.

When Barry got home, a wave of exhaustion came over him. He put it down to the terrible events of the afternoon and went straight to bed. In the middle of the night, however, he was awoken by a tiny LED pulsating beneath the sheet. At first, he thought it might be one of the government's surveillance cockroaches, but instead he discovered a light on his own leg above what looked like a hinged rectangle covering, which, when opened, revealed a battery inside. Barry was horrified and understood at once what had happened. He was one of the doppelgangers and it was very likely that he had killed the original Barry by mistake.

Next morning over a breakfast of boiled eggs and soldiers, Barry couldn't look real Barry's parents in the eyes. He knew that what he had done was so abhorrent that he'd never be forgiven, and rightly so, but he also knew that he could not sustain the lie, either practically or ethically. The lives of real Barry's family were ruined, he was sure of it. Not only had they lost a much-loved only child, but paranoia and doubt would also likely infect them. How long had they loved an imposter? They wouldn't be able to trust themselves or each other, perhaps worrying that they too might be electronic automatons. Even though electronic Barry was made of cogs, wires and circuits, he knew that the only way he

could avert their suffering was if they could not feel the pain; and the only way he could ensure that was if they no longer existed.

Electronic Barry didn't need to think twice; it was as if he were programmed to reach for the nearest hard metal object, which happened to be an egg spoon. He attacked real Barry's parents with such ferocious precision that they didn't have time to utter a single sound.

Drenched in the blood of real Barry's dead parents, electronic Barry sat down to finish his boiled egg. Moments later, the door bell rang. Barry peered around the door jamb and saw, through the mottled glass of the front door, real Barry's maternal grandparents. Electronic Barry reasoned that, just as he had effectively and conclusively eliminated real Barry's parents' faculties for pain and distress, he must now do the same for Barry's grandparents, both maternal and paternal, as well as uncles, aunts, cousins, friends and friends of friends, all of whom would be distraught when they learned about the fate that had befallen their loved ones.

Barry had set in motion a process that had the potential to affect every living, sentient thing with a capacity to love and feel pain. He understood that he had two choices: he must either halt this snowballing situation now or see it through to its logical conclusion…

Twenty-seven years later, electronic Barry had benevolently eradicated every human being on planet Earth, as well as twenty-two billion pets (not including tropical fish, tortoises and cats who don't care one way or the other). The human race was extinct and over the subsequent millennia every record or sign of mankind slowly turned to dust.

Epilogue

██████████ says: "This is why it's unhealthy to eat snacks between meals. Not only is it the leading cause of tooth decay, it could mean the extermination of the human race."

ARE YOU TRUTH BLIND?

Did you know that people's minds can be conditioned so that they, and only they, can see certain colours?

Please note: those of you who rejected our kind offer to join the OTG (Officist Truth Group*) and attend our truth-conditioning workshops will NOT be able to see the hidden words in this fun puzzle.

It's a shame that those who deny the OTG and its doctrines will miss out on this, and all future, recreational opportunities.

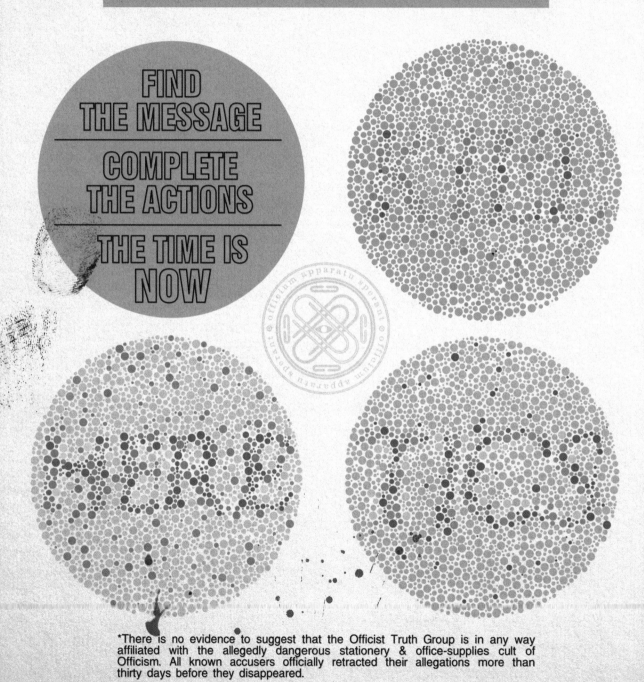

FIND THE MESSAGE

COMPLETE THE ACTIONS

THE TIME IS NOW

WARNING: HEAVY-HANDED METAPHOR

Tomorrow it's my turn for the Trials.
What will be my fate?
Why haven't you found me?
Have we been forgotten??

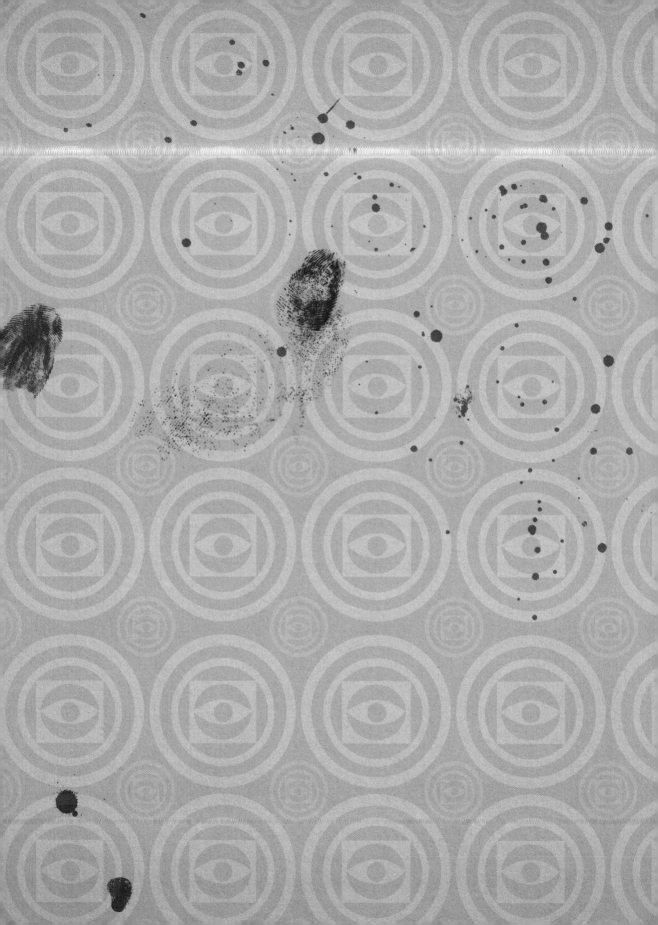